ALSO BY FREIDA MCFADDEN

ONE
BY
ONE

ONE
BY
ONE

FREIDA McFADDEN

Poisoned Pen
PRESS

Published by Poisoned Pen Press, an imprint of Sourcebooks
P.O. Box 4410, Naperville, Illinois 60567-4410
(630) 961-3900
sourcebooks.com

Originally self-published in 2020 by Freida McFadden.

Cataloging-in-Publication Data is on file with the Library of Congress.

Printed and bound in the United States of America.
LSC 10 9 8 7 6 5 4 3

To Libby and Melanie (as always)

PROLOGUE

There will be six of us.

Six adults. Stuffed into a six-person minivan like sardines, with all the luggage we felt we couldn't possibly live without during our vacation at a swanky luxury inn. Our reservation is for six days. Six days of hiking and hot tubs. Six days away from civilization.

My mother was a religious woman. That's how I know that on the sixth day, both man and serpent were created. You know—the snake that eventually convinced Adam and Eve to eat the forbidden fruit and got them kicked out of the Garden of Eden forever? That's why the number six represents both man and the evil that weakens him.

In Revelation, 666 is the number of the devil.

The sixth commandment is thou shalt not kill.

Six is not a nice number.

I'm not religious. I don't go to church. I don't believe in a higher power. Six is just like any other number to me.

But I know that every single one of these six people has a secret they don't want anyone to know.

I can tell you my secret right now:

At the end of this week, only one of us will make it home alive.

CHAPTER 1

CLAIRE

I don't know when I started to hate my husband.

I didn't always. When we tied the knot, over ten years ago, we held hands and I swore I would love him forever. Until death did us part. And I *meant* it. I meant it with every fiber of my being. I genuinely believed I would be married to Noah Matchett for the rest of my life. I fantasized about the two of us growing old together— holding hands while sitting in matching rocking chairs in a retirement home. And when the minister declared us husband and wife, I patted myself on the back for choosing the right guy.

I'm not sure what happened between then and now. But I can't stand the guy anymore.

"Where's my UChicago shirt, Claire?"

Noah is hunched over the top drawer of his dresser, his hazel eyes staring down into the contents of the drawer. He clears his throat, which is what he always does when he's concentrating hard on something. I used to find it cute and endearing. Now I find it irritating. Nails-on-a-chalkboard irritating.

"I don't know." I grab a couple of shirts out of my own dresser drawer and shove them into the brown luggage gaping open on our bed. "It's not in the drawer?"

He looks up and purses his lips. "If it were in the drawer, why would I be asking you about it?"

Hmm. Maybe this is why I hate my husband. Because he's become a huge jerk.

"I don't know where your shirt is." I start sifting through my bras. How many bras do you bring for a weeklong trip? I'm never certain. "It's *your* shirt."

"Yeah, but *you* did the laundry."

"So?" I stuff four bras into my luggage—that should be enough. "Do you think while I'm doing laundry, I'm thinking to myself, 'Oh, here's Noah's UChicago shirt. Better put that somewhere special instead of the drawer where I put every other shirt of his I've ever washed in the history of doing laundry'?"

He rolls his eyes at me and sifts through the drawer one more time. "Well, it's not in here."

"I don't know what to tell you, Noah."

He rubs at the dark stubble on his chin that has a hint of gray. He hasn't shaved in three days because he's been working from home. He doesn't care what he looks like unless he has to go to work. "Maybe you put it in Aidan's dresser by mistake?"

That's unlikely, since our nine-year-old son now does his own laundry. Somehow, my fourth grader can wash his own clothes, but my adult husband is incapable of it. From the moment we got married, laundry automatically became my responsibility. There was no discussion. The wife does the laundry. End of story.

"You're welcome to check Aidan's dresser," I say.

Noah shoots me an exasperated look, then he stomps off in the direction of our son's room, his large feet creaking against the floorboards. He's not going to find the shirt there. I would bet a million bucks the shirt is right in that top drawer where he's been looking all along.

In only a few short hours, we are embarking on a weeklong trip to a cozy inn located in the northern part of Colorado. It will be about a four-hour drive to get there, followed by a week of breakfast buffets, a Jacuzzi, nature walks, and a lake with trout that are basically jumping out of the water. It's the perfect combination of getting away from urban (or in our case, suburban) life and still enjoying hot and cold running water and cable TV. I can't wait.

Well, except for the four hours in a car with my husband. Who probably won't stop talking about his stupid UChicago shirt.

I drop a handful of socks into my luggage and walk over to Noah's dresser. I've got two full dressers and a closet filled with clothes, whereas Noah just has the one dresser and a few dress shirts in the closet. When we were first together, he used to tease me about how much clothing I had compared with him. He still teases me about it, but now the jabs are considerably less playful.

If you buy one more shirt, we're going to have to buy a separate house just for your clothing, Claire.

It's not so much. My friend Lindsay literally has an *entire room* just for her clothing. But she's not married. So she gets to do whatever she wants without another person criticizing her every move.

I sift through the drawer, pushing through the range of gray and black T-shirts. Noah has never been a fan of

5

bright colors. He tends to stick with the grayscale. One time, he bought a green shirt. That was his midlife crisis.

After only a few seconds, I see the flash of maroon shoved into one corner of the drawer. I pull out the shirt and see the word UChicago etched across the front in faded lettering. Noah has had this T-shirt as long as I've known him. It's his favorite shirt.

For a moment, I'm seized with the urge to stuff this shirt into the bottom of the trash can without telling him. He'll go nuts looking for it. And really, this shirt needs to be retired. There's a hole forming at the collar and the hem is all frayed.

Then again, I've got enough secrets from my husband right now. And I don't want to miss out on the pure satisfaction of informing him that the shirt was in the drawer all along.

"Mommy?"

My seven-year-old daughter, Emma, is standing at the doorway to our bedroom, watching me contemplate what to do with her father's favorite T-shirt. Even though we've already had breakfast, she's still wearing her *Frozen* pajamas, which are royal blue with little snowflakes all over them. I guiltily shove the T-shirt back into the drawer and turn to smile at Emma. She doesn't smile back.

While her big brother is excited about the idea of staying with Aunt Penny for a week, Emma is decidedly freaked out. For the last week, she has crawled into our queen-size bed every single night to sleep. Fortunately, Noah and I sleep with a gap the size of the Atlantic Ocean between us.

"What's wrong, honey?" I ask.

Emma's lower lip trembles. She runs over to me

and wraps her skinny arms around my hips. "Don't go, Mommy. *Please*."

"Emma…"

I attempt to pry her off me, but she's stuck like glue. It's sweet. As much as I dislike my husband, I love my children. I've always loved children. It's part of the reason I became a teacher. Nothing makes me happier than seeing the smiles light up those little faces.

I reach down and wipe Emma's damp, light-brown curls from her face. Her hair looks like mine, but it's still baby soft. I lean in and bury my face in it—it smells like her watermelon shampoo. "It's just a week, sweetheart," I say.

She looks up at me with her little tear-streaked cheeks. "But what if something happens to you?"

I don't know how my seven-year-old daughter got so neurotic. She worries about everything, including things no child has any business worrying about. Like when there was talk of a teacher strike last year, she was worried I wouldn't have a job and we wouldn't be able to afford food. What seven-year-old worries about that?

"Why are you so worried, Emma?"

She chews on her little pink lip. "Well, you're going to be in the woods."

I don't blame her for worrying if that's what she thinks. Neither of her parents is what you would call the "outdoorsy type" by any stretch of the imagination. "Don't worry," I say. "We're staying in a nice hotel. It will be really safe."

Her light-brown eyebrows bunch together. "But I had a dream that…"

"That what?"

Emma scrunches up her face. "That a monster in the forest ate you up!"

It's laughable, of course. We'll be sticking to the hotel and its amenities most of the week, and if we do venture out, we will keep to circumscribed locations like hiking trails for city-slicker tourists. And even if we weren't, I'm sure whatever Emma is imagining is some sort of blue Cookie Monster–like creature appearing out of the wilderness and stuffing us all into his mouth in one fell swoop.

Yet Emma does sometimes have a strange intuition about things. One night, she came into our bedroom at two in the morning, crying about a dream that Grandpa Joe had died. Two days later, my seemingly healthy father succumbed to a massive heart attack. Noah chalked it all up to coincidence, but I never forgot.

As much as I hate to admit it, Emma's premonition is making me uneasy. Maybe this trip is a mistake.

I look down at the two sets of luggage on our bed. Noah's with the clothes stuffed haphazardly inside, and mine with everything folded neatly. What if I told him I didn't want to go? Would he freak out? Or would he be relieved that he doesn't have to spend the next week with someone he hates?

But then I hear Noah's laughter coming from outside the door. Apparently, he heard the whole exchange. "Emma!" He stands in the doorway with his arms folded across his chest. "You're not really worried about that, are you?"

Emma's lower lip trembles.

"You know there's no such thing as monsters!" He cocks his head to the side. "Well, except for…tickle monsters!"

Despite her worries, Emma's brown eyes widen

excitedly. After a solid minute of tickling, she appears to have forgotten all about her scary dream. It must be nice to be a child, who can live in the moment and forget everything with the help of a little tickling.

Noah is good with the kids. I can't say he isn't. They adore him, and he loves them as much as I do. And that's why we're still together, even though we despise each other. Even though we've never said the words out loud, we both know we're staying together for the kids. For now.

"Okay," Noah says to Emma. "Your aunt Penny is going to be here any minute. Is your suitcase all packed?"

We bought Emma a *Frozen* rolling suitcase just for this trip. She was so excited about it when she got it. "Almost."

"Well, you better finish getting packed." He arches one eyebrow. "Or else...the tickle monster might come back."

He makes his fingers into claws, and Emma squeals and flees the room. He watches her go, a crooked smile on his face. For a moment, I recall how much I used to love him. How much fun we used to have together. The way my whole body would tingle in anticipation when I knew he was taking me out to dinner. He used to make me laugh the same way he made Emma laugh.

I wonder if we could fix things. Maybe if I say something kind right now instead of my usual snarky comment, he would smile and laugh. And maybe we could use this trip as a chance to heal our relationship. Maybe it isn't too late for us.

But then Noah turns to look at me, and the smile slides off his face.

"You lost my shirt," he says.

"It was right in your drawer all along, Einstein."

We are not going to be fixing things today. Or ever.

CHAPTER 2

CLAIRE

My sister Penny arrives in our driveway at promptly half past nine to get the kids. My easygoing firstborn, Aidan, accepts a kiss on the cheek, then obediently climbs into her SUV and buckles himself in. He only recently graduated from having a booster seat, and he takes the responsibility very seriously.

Emma is a different story. She attaches herself firmly to my hip, any comfort she had derived from the tickle attack now long faded.

Penny comes around the side of the CR-V, her blond ponytail swinging as she wipes her hands on her yoga pants. "What's the problem, Em? You don't want to spend a super fun week with Aunt Penny?"

Emma will have a great time with Penny. Penny has three kids of her own, and they are always elbow-deep in some exciting (and messy) baking project. Or art involving macaroni. And she's got a freaking Slip 'N Slide in her backyard. But right now, my daughter couldn't care less. She responds by burrowing her head deeper into my belly.

"She had a dream that a monster ate us," I explain.

"Oh, scary!" Penny nods sympathetically. "But I don't think there are any monsters where your mom and dad are going, Em. They're going to north Colorado, and all the monsters are in the south. So they should be fine."

Another kid might have been persuaded, but Emma is the daughter of a physicist. She has an impeccable sense of logic. So she just shoots Penny a withering look and returns her face to my hip.

For the second time this morning, I wonder if this trip is a mistake. I'm already fighting with Noah, and now we're going to spend *four hours* together in the car. Sometimes having our friends in the car with us dampens our fights, but often they are just an embarrassing public audience to how much Noah and I have grown to hate each other.

Maybe I should stay home. It's not too late to back out. Noah can go without me.

Then again, there's another reason why I want to go on this trip. And anyway, the reservation is nonrefundable.

Working together, Penny and I manage to pry Emma off my hip, mostly with the promise of lots and lots of ice cream. We throw the kids' luggage into her trunk, then they're ready to go. I get a jab of sadness in my chest, knowing I'll be away from my babies for a whole week. Even though we take a trip every year, it's always painful.

"I'll take good care of them," Penny promises.

"Thanks." I know she will. She's like a supermom. Between my constant arguments with Noah and my busy job as a special-ed teacher, sometimes I feel like I'm falling short in the motherhood department. But I would never give up my job—I love it too much.

"By the way," she says, lowering her voice a notch, "did you tell Noah about…?"

I glance at the house. Noah is still packing upstairs in our bedroom. "No. Not yet."

Her eyes widen. "Claire, you have to tell him! When are you going to say something?"

"Soon, okay?" I don't want to explain about our stupid fight over his T-shirt. "I'll tell him before we get there."

She flashes me her classic I'm-the-big-sister-who-knows-better-than-you look. I hate that look. Especially because she's right. Noah and I need to have a talk ASAP. I can't blindside him on this.

"I'll tell him as soon as we get into the car," I say. "Before we get Lindsay."

Yes, that should make for an interesting ride.

I hug Penny goodbye and fold myself in half to lean into the back seat to kiss the kids one last time. Emma clings to me extra hard. Why can't I push away this sick feeling? We've gone on a trip like this every single year we've been married. This is the first time I've had such a bad feeling about it.

It's all Emma's stupid dream. I know it's ridiculous, but it's weighing on me.

I need to put it out of my head. Before I let it ruin the week.

CHAPTER 3

CLAIRE

We're taking my silver minivan on the trip because it will hold all six of us. Noah thought I was being ridiculous when I bought the minivan, but I'm constantly driving car pool, so it's come in handy a lot. There are three rows of seats, so the kids don't have to be squashed on top of each other. I love it. As usual, Noah was absolutely wrong.

I remove Emma's booster seat so all the adults will have a place to sit. Last night, I cleaned out the car, which was embarrassingly dirty. How did so many french fries get in the back seat? And why was everything so *sticky* back there? I did the best I could to clean it up, but there are probably still a few sticky patches left.

We each have one piece of luggage, but my bag is twice the size of Noah's and stuffed to the breaking point. He tosses my luggage into the back so roughly that I'm glad I didn't pack anything fragile. He's decided to take out his aggression toward me on my luggage. On the plus side, at least he shaved for the trip.

"What the hell do you need so much stuff for?" he grumbles. "We're only going for a week."

Admittedly, I didn't pack light. But it's the end of June, which means it could just as easily be chilly as it could be sweltering. I have to be prepared. "You brought plenty too," I point out.

Noah gently places his brand-new tackle box into the back. "I'm going fishing. I have to have supplies."

Right. He's been excited about going fishing for months. "I still don't get why you're so excited about sitting on a lake for hours. It sounds excruciating."

He shrugs. "I just…I need to clear my head."

Fine, whatever. As long as he doesn't ask me to go with him. If the two of us go out on a boat into the middle of the lake, I have a bad feeling only one of us will come back alive.

Noah takes the spare car keys from the pocket of his jeans and slides into the driver's seat. It's a strange move, considering this is *my* car. I rap on the driver's-side window. "What do you think you're doing?"

"What? Aren't we going?"

"Yeah, but it's my car. Why are *you* driving?"

He gives me a pointed look. "Come on, Claire. You've had this car for three years, and there are already, like, ten dents in it."

That's not entirely inaccurate. Still. "Not all those dents are my fault."

"Whatever you say."

I grit my teeth, wondering if this is worth fighting about. It's not like I love to drive or am so eager to be behind the wheel for four hours. But why does he assume he's always going to be the one driving during these long trips? Worse, he's going to complain later about how I made him do all the driving and now he's tired and crabby.

If we didn't have two children together, I would call it quits right now. Right this minute.

For a moment, I allow myself to fantasize. *Noah, it's over.* It would feel so good to say those words.

Instead, I climb into the passenger's seat beside him. I smooth out the light pink shorts I bought last week that show off what I think are still some pretty nice legs for my age. Not that Noah would notice. He used to dress nicely when we went out together, but now he sticks to jeans and a T-shirt. Although I admit they don't look bad on his solid frame.

He pushes his glasses up his nose and swivels his head to look at me. "Aren't you going to use the bathroom?"

"No."

He frowns. "Look, you should go now. I'm not stopping in thirty minutes at a gas station so you can go."

"Fine. I won't have to go."

"Really? Because I feel like whenever you don't go right before we leave, I end up having to stop right away."

I glare at him. Are we really having this conversation? I'm not five years old. "Noah, if I needed to use the bathroom, I would go. I don't have to go."

He stares at me for a moment, then turns his key in the ignition. "Whatever you say, Claire."

I drop back in my seat, fuming, as he carefully backs out of the driveway and starts driving in the direction of Lindsay's house. After a minute of silence, he hits the button to start the radio, and Adam Levine's voice croons the lyrics to a song I've heard hundreds of times before.

Noah stares out at the road through his glasses. Back

when we first started dating, he only wore glasses in class and when he was driving. He never wore them on our dates. Over the last fifteen years, he's gotten to the point where he wears them all the time. He says his vision has gotten worse, but I'm not so sure. He wears them all the time for the same reason he doesn't bother to shave anymore if he doesn't have to be at work. I'm lucky he gets dressed or showers anymore.

"I got us separate rooms," I blurt out.

Noah slides his foot onto the brake at a red light. He turns to stare at me, his eyes wide. "*What?*"

"At the inn." I look away from him, out the windshield. "I booked us two separate bedrooms."

"You did?" Even though we have been fighting nonstop all morning (hell, all *year*), he sounds hurt. "But… why?"

"Well…" I play with a loose thread on my shirt. "I just thought… I mean, you snore, Noah. And you're always saying how I move around too much in my sleep. So I thought maybe, you know, we could both get a better night's sleep if we're apart." I hastily add, "Just for the week."

I hazard a look at Noah. His eyes are pinned on the crosswalk, and a muscle twitches in his jaw.

"I mean," I babble on, "there are a lot of couples that take separate vacations *entirely*. There's nothing wrong with it. You know, a little time apart. You're going to be spending most of your time fishing anyway, and you'll have to get up real early…"

The light turns green, and Noah hits the gas so hard that my head snaps back. "Right. I get it."

"So…you're okay with it?"

That muscle is still twitching in his jaw. "Of course. Separate bedrooms. Perfect. Maybe we won't have to see each other at all during this trip."

"Noah…"

But before I can say another word, Noah reaches over and turns up the volume of the radio loud enough to drown out any attempt at conversation. I guess we're done discussing this.

He's not thrilled. Frankly, I thought there was a chance he might be relieved we wouldn't be stuck in a tiny room together for a whole week. Apparently not.

Still, I'm not going to take it back. I've been looking forward to these separate rooms all month. I probably should've told him sooner, but I didn't want to have to deal with him sulking about it for weeks. I'm sure once we're there, he'll see the wisdom in my decision. And maybe next year, we *will* end up taking separate vacations. Lindsay and I could take that trip to Hawaii we've been talking about for ages.

Or maybe next year, we won't be together anymore at all. You never know.

CHAPTER 4

CLAIRE

It takes nearly half an hour to drive from our house in Castle Pines to Lindsay's apartment building in Denver, during which time Noah and I fail to exchange a single word. He won't even look at me.

The logical part of me is saying that we should call off this trip. Or at least, I should back out. The four-hour drive is bad enough, but now we have to spend an entire *week* together without the buffer of our work and the children? It sounds like hell.

Then again, I have my reasons for wanting to go.

The plan is that we're all going to meet in front of Lindsay's building, because it's a place where everyone can park easily for the week. We're ten minutes early, but Lindsay is already standing outside her building with two huge pieces of luggage—more than I've got. I consider pointing that out to Noah, but I decide not to break our code of silence.

Lindsay waves enthusiastically when she sees the minivan. She looks fantastic. Her blond hair is pulled into a perfectly messy bun, she's got a pair of Ray-Bans on her nose, and her skinny jeans are tucked into the cutest pair of black hiking boots. I'd like to think I have kept in good shape since college, but of the group of us, Lindsay is the only one who looks *better* than she did in college. It's like her butt gets higher every year.

I glance over at Noah to see if he's giving her a once-over. He isn't. He's still sulking about our conversation.

We pop the trunk for Lindsay to throw her bags inside, then she slides into the middle row, right behind me. We do a quick seat hug, and Noah breaks his silence to say hello. Even though Noah has known Lindsay nearly as long as I have, they don't hug. Noah isn't the kind of guy who goes around hugging people left and right—hugs are reserved for close family only.

"So!" I say. "We finally get to meet Warner! *Very* exciting!"

Lindsay's porcelain skin flushes with happiness. "I can't wait for you to meet him, Claire. He's…well, he's amazing. I really think he's the one."

"Is this the doctor?" Noah asks. He sounds utterly disinterested, but at least he's being polite.

She tucks a loose strand of her ash-blond hair behind her ear. "He's a *surgeon*."

I can see him eyeing her in the rearview mirror. "What kind of surgeon?"

"A plastic surgeon." Before Noah can comment, she quickly adds, "But he doesn't just do boob jobs and face-lifts. He does facial reconstructions. He works *miracles*. You should hear what his patients say about him online." She flops back against the seat. "But he's not full of himself at all. He's really sweet and down-to-earth."

I wink at her. "And cute?"

"So cute!" She giggles. "And you know what the best part is? He's a Scorpio."

Noah lets out a loud snort. "*That's* the best part?"

Noah doesn't believe in horoscopes or zodiac signs or anything that doesn't have rigorous experimental evidence behind it. He's not shy about saying so either. It doesn't bother Lindsay though. According to her, he's a typical Capricorn.

"It's perfect because I'm a Virgo," she explains to him. "Virgo is an earth sign, and we are the pickiest of the earth signs. But water signs, like Scorpio, soften us up and give us an emotional outlet." She regards us solemnly. "It's a very powerful balance."

"I see," he mutters. "So how is it that such an eligible young Scorpio finds himself still single?"

She furrows her brow. "It's sort of a sad story. Warner was with a woman for the last seven years, but a year ago, she…died."

I clasp a hand over my mouth. "Oh, that's terrible."

She nods soberly. "Cancer. It was very hard on him."

"Of course."

"So…we've been taking it kind of slow." She glances out the window. "But things are getting pretty serious now. He was even hinting at looking for rings the other day."

"Wow," I breathe. "That's incredible. I wasn't even sure you wanted to get married."

"I wasn't sure either," she admits. "But Warner is just so amazing. Ever since I met him, it's like I can't imagine ever being with anyone else. But I'm sure you know what that's like."

I suck in a breath. I glance over at Noah, and it's pretty clear he's thinking what I'm thinking.

"Ooh, there he is!" Lindsay squeals.

I snap my head up and follow Lindsay's gaze out the window. She's been telling me about this guy for the last six months, but she's never let me meet him, and she's been pretty stingy with the details. So none of my internet searches turned up anything, and I've been dying to meet the guy.

And now that I've finally seen Warner, well…

Let's just say that this is exactly the sort of guy I would've imagined Lindsay would finally decide to marry.

First of all, he's gorgeous. So gorgeous that I find my jaw dropping open a little bit. Not that Noah isn't a decent-looking guy—my husband can be downright handsome on the rare occasion he puts on a suit and tie. But Warner looks like he could be a movie star. Sun-streaked blond hair, clear blue eyes, bulging muscles visible under his fitted T-shirt. And he has a chin cleft. Lindsay loves chin clefts. She has this theory that every truly good-looking person has a chin cleft.

"Wow," I say aloud.

"I know, right?" Lindsay looks pleased by my approval. "Isn't he hot?"

Noah is rolling his eyes next to me, but even he has to realize how gorgeous Warner is. When I look back at Lindsay, I can see how smitten she is. She's always been the pickiest person I know when it comes to men—she has dropped a lot of perfectly good ones for no discernible reason—but I have to admit, she knew what she was doing when she held out. She really likes this guy.

The other thing I notice about Warner is that he only has one piece of luggage. One small bag. Noah packed pretty light, but this guy wins. All he's got is a single, small duffel bag that looks like it could only fit maybe a day or two worth of clothing.

Lindsay opens the rear door, and Warner ducks into the van. He flashes a smile that makes him look even more attractive, if that were even possible. He holds out his hand to me—his handshake is warm and firm. If this man were my surgeon, I would feel like I was in very capable hands. He could suck fat out of my love handles any day of the week.

"You must be Claire," Warner says. His voice is a rich baritone that reverberates within the car. "I've heard so much about you."

"All good, I hope!" My voice trembles a bit. I'm oddly nervous.

"Exclusively." He winks at me, which makes me titter like a schoolgirl. He turns his attention to Noah. "Noah, right?"

Noah shakes his outstretched hand with considerably less enthusiasm. "Nice to meet you. You're the one who recommended this inn, weren't you?"

Warner nods energetically. "I've stayed there many times before. You're going to love it. I heard you were interested in going fishing?"

Noah shrugs, even though it's all he could talk about for the last week. "I thought I might give it a try."

"The fishing is great out there. The trout are jumping out of the water. You'll love it."

Lindsay reaches for Warner's hand, and she slides her fingers into his. He grins at her with lust in his eyes. They make a very attractive couple. I pretend not to watch. I certainly don't want to admit the whole thing makes my chest burn with jealousy. Noah and I used to be that way. But that's just a distant memory.

As Lindsay and Warner get all cuddly in the back seat, I stare out the window, wondering where Jack and Michelle are. Michelle is always very prompt, but Jack sometimes makes the two of them late. I glance at the back seat, hoping they arrive before Lindsay and Warner start outright making out. He is stroking her chin, and I'm worried it's not far off.

"So how did the two of you meet again?" I ask loudly.

Lindsay breaks away from Warner, her eyes bright. "Oh, it's a great story! We were at the supermarket. I had just checked out and was carrying two bags of groceries to my car, and wouldn't you know it—the bottom fell out of one of the bags!"

The corner of Warner's lips quirks up. "They always overpack the bags at that supermarket."

She tilts her head affectionately in his direction. "Anyway, he was right behind me and he helped me to get all the groceries to my car." She giggles. "Even though I later found out he was on his way to do surgery and I made him late!"

He throws an arm around her and pulls her close. "It was just a boob job. Not life or death."

Lindsay is positively beaming. She loves a good meet-cute. She has been convinced none of her prior relationships worked out because they didn't have a good story about how they met. Now, finally, she's got her great meet-cute.

For a second, I catch Noah's smirk, but then he quickly looks away. Noah and I don't have a great meet-cute story. We met because he lived down the hall from me junior year of college. We didn't so much meet as we saw each other around a lot over the first half of the year.

He often helped me carry heavy packages up to my room. I guess that's sort of romantic. Usually, after he helped me with my packages, we would chat in my room for a while. One day, he had just carried up a care package from my mother, and after he set the box down on my desk, he rubbed at the back of his neck and flashed me a crooked smile. "You want to grab some dinner?" he asked.

"Thai?" I asked.

"Great!" he said. I only found out later he hates Thai food.

I hadn't been looking for any sort of relationship at the time. I had one serious boyfriend the year before, but it ended abruptly when I caught him cheating on me. We had actually been thinking about getting back together over the summer, but then I found out he drowned tragically when he was away at some summer program, and the whole experience left me shaken and reluctant to get involved again. But Noah and I had a great time at dinner. I always knew he was smart, but I didn't realize how funny he was. And cute. Still, I thought we were just friends. Until he walked me home and he kissed me in front of our dorm.

I remember being surprised at how well he kissed. I had kissed a few boys before, and it was always okay, but with Noah, it was on another level. Until that night, I had thought of him as my somewhat dorky neighbor, so this was an extremely pleasant surprise. And then the way he looked at me when he pulled away... I knew right then that if he asked me out a second time, I would say yes.

I look over at Noah now. When was the last time he kissed me like that? I can't even remember. I'm pretty sure it will never happen again.

A rap on the passenger-side window jolts me out of

my thoughts. Jack and Michelle Alpert are right outside the car, trying to get our attention. Jack is waving wildly. And then he mouths the word "Sorry."

Finally! They're almost ten minutes late.

Noah unlocks the rear door, and Jack wrenches it open. "You're late," Noah snaps at him.

"Good to see you too, buddy," Jack says.

Noah has to get out to help them squeeze their luggage into the back. Noah and Jack usually joke around a lot when they get together, but Noah seems too tense for that now. Like Lindsay and me, Noah and Jack were roommates back in college. It's an opposites-attract sort of situation because the two of them are very different. Noah was the physics nerd, whereas Jack had long hair and played the guitar. When he strummed at that guitar, singing old Beatles songs, my knees got weak. Even now, he's got that rugged look—his hair is still shaggy compared with Noah's and Warner's, and his hands are calloused from manual labor and playing the guitar.

Something I never told Noah is that between the two cute guys who lived next door to me during my junior year, *Jack* was the one I had been hoping would ask me out. And later in the year, at a party where we both had too much to drink, Jack admitted he had wanted to ask me out, but he chickened out and Noah got to me first. As we both sipped our rum and cokes, he grinned and asked if I thought there was any chance I might ever want to switch.

I was slightly drunk, but I still said no. I was not interested in switching. No way. I loved *Noah*. At that point, even though we had been dating only a few months, I was beginning to think he was the man I wanted to spend my life with.

What a mistake.

Michelle slides into the back seat first. Her jet-black hair is pulled into a flawless bun, and she's wearing a crisp, fitted white T-shirt that looks like she ironed it this morning. I don't think I've ever seen her with one hair out of place. She works as a divorce lawyer, and rumor has it she's the best divorce attorney in all of Denver. If Noah and I end up going in that direction, it's going to be a race to see which one of us can retain her services. She's the opposite of Jack in a lot of ways, but they've always seemed happy together.

Maybe it's because they don't have children. According to Jack, Michelle has never been interested in having kids. So they've never had the vicious argument at two in the morning over whose turn it is to get up with the screaming baby. Or fight number 179 over who's changing the poopy diaper.

"Sorry we were late." Michelle crosses her legs as she shoots Jack a look. "I caught this one trying to pack a *gun*."

"Jack!" Lindsay gasps.

"Jesus Christ." Jack runs a hand through his shaggy dark hair. "I wasn't packing a handgun. It was a *rifle*. I heard there's a place to go hunting over there."

"That doesn't make it any better, Jack," Michelle says sharply. I feel sorry for him, trying to best her in an argument. It must be impossible.

"Hunting is barbaric," Lindsay sniffs.

Jack makes a face at her. "You eat meat, don't you, Lindsay? How do you think it gets to your plate? Do you think those animals die of natural causes?"

"It's different when you're hunting," Lindsay says. "Have you ever seen *Bambi*? Remember when the hunter shot Bambi's mother? Is that what you want, Jack? To be the one who kills Bambi's mother?"

One corner of Jack's lips tugs upward. "Don't be fooled. If a deer had the chance, it would kill you and everyone you care about." Michelle pokes Jack in the ribs and he yelps in pain. "I thought it was something we could do together, Michelle."

"You *know* I've got a ton of work to do during this trip," Michelle sighs. "I'll be lucky if I leave the room except for meals. But even if I didn't, I would *never* go hunting. Ever."

And now everyone is glaring at Jack.

"Look," Jack says, "I didn't bring the gun. I'm not going to kill Bambi's mother. Let's just get going."

"Great idea," Noah says. And once again, he hits the gas so hard that my neck snaps back.

CHAPTER 5

ANONYMOUS

The thing I remember most about my childhood is my mom's car.

It was a green Dodge with a long scratch on the passenger side and a big dent in the front fender. She got it used before I can remember—that car was older than I was. She used to tell me how my dad went with her to the used-car lot and negotiated with the sleazy salesman to get her a good deal. My dad was a salesman too. That's how he knew the tricks. That's also why he traveled so much.

My dad bought a car seat for the back when I was a little kid. He used to make a big deal about strapping me inside. "You all snug and safe back there, sport?" he would ask.

But when my father went away on his trips, my mother would get depressed. She didn't give a shit if I was strapped in snug and safe. When we went out, she said to get in the back and gave me ten seconds to get my seat belt on. If the seat belt wasn't on by then, too damn bad. *You think I have time to wait the rest of the day for you to strap yourself in?*

Mostly, she would take me to the grocery store. She didn't take me to friends' houses, playgrounds, or anywhere fun. Just grocery stores. Or the gas station.

When I was four years old, when my dad was out of town, she took me out in the car. I couldn't get the car seat buckled on my own so I just sat next to it in the back, behind the driver seat. The strap on the seat belt went over my neck and cut into the skin. I knew better than to complain.

When we got to the grocery store, I started to follow her, but she shook her head. "I just need to get a few things," she told me as she hung her big purple purse over her shoulder. "You stay in the car. I don't need you slowing me down."

Then she closed the door to the car with me inside.

She had left me in the car before. Lots of times. But today was hot. Hot enough that everyone on the street was wearing shorts and wifebeaters and fanning themselves as they talked about how damn hot it was.

When my mom was in the car, the air conditioner was going. You could barely feel it in the back, but it was circulating. Unfortunately, after she killed the engine, the temperature in the car started to go up.

At first, it wasn't too bad. Hot, but I didn't mind hot. Then it got hotter. So hot it was hard to breathe. You know why it's hard to breathe when it's hot? Heat causes molecules to disperse, so each breath takes in less oxygen.

I was suffocating.

She said she would be right back. As I waited, it became clear it wasn't going to be a quick grocery trip like she promised. But if I got out of the car, there would be consequences. Bad consequences.

So I sat there, the sweat beading on my forehead. And my eyes drifted shut.

I was jarred awake by pounding on my window. It was a woman about my mother's age. I lifted my head and blinked my bleary eyes. The woman was yelling. "Are you okay? Can you open the door?"

I didn't know what to do. My mom would be angry if I opened the door. But this woman kept pounding on the window. My head hurt. So I unlocked the car, and before I knew it, the woman was wrenching the door open.

Even though it was at least ninety degrees outside, the fresh air felt good. I took a gulp of air.

"Oh my God," the woman was saying as she unbuckled my seat belt and pulled me from the car. I weighed very little, even for my age, and she lifted me easily. "Are you okay? Can you say anything?"

There was concern in her eyes. My mom never looked like that. Too bad this woman couldn't take me home. I could be her kid instead. "I'm okay."

"What the hell do you think you're doing?" My mother's voice rang out across the parking lot. "What are you doing to my child?"

My mother and the woman started yelling at each other. The woman was saying I could have died. My mother told her to mind her own damn business. The woman said she was going to report my mother. Finally, my mom shoved me back into the Dodge and we took off before I had a chance to get my seat belt buckled again.

"What did you unlock the door for?" she snapped at me.

"It was hot."

"Well, I hope it was worth it. Now she's going to report me for being a terrible parent and you're going to get taken away from us. They'll **put you in** a foster home. You'll never see me or your father **again**."

The thought of never seeing **my mom** again? Not so bad. But the thought of never **seeing** my father again made me sick. So sick, I had to **make** her pull over so I could vomit.

CHAPTER 6

CLAIRE

Here's my dilemma:

I have to pee. Urgently. I'm worried one violent sneeze might result in a tragedy.

Except we are less than one hour into our journey, so how can I ask Noah to stop to use the bathroom? He's going to say, "I told you so." And he's not going to say it in a teasing way. He's going to say it in a mean, patronizing way in front of four of my friends. And he will hold it over my head for the next several hours, if not for the rest of our lives.

I look at the gas gauge. It's hovering a little below half. Maybe I can spin this.

"I think we should get some gas," I announce.

Noah looks down at the gauge in astonishment. "What are you talking about? We have plenty of gas. The tank is half full."

"Well, it's half *empty*." I cough. "And the minivan goes through gas really quickly. You don't know, Noah. This is *my* car."

He narrows his eyes at me. "You need to use the bathroom, don't you?"

I let out a huff. "I don't know what you're talking about. Why are you so obsessed with me needing the bathroom?"

"Because…" His knuckles whiten on the steering wheel. "We've barely gotten on the highway and now we're already going to have to stop. I *told* you to use the bathroom before we left. You *always* do this."

"But I don't need the bathroom. I think we should get some gas, that's all."

"We can get gas in an hour or two when we stop for lunch."

An hour or two? My bladder will have exploded by then. Why did I drink so much water with breakfast? "We don't want to run out of gas on the highway." I point to a sign on the road. "There's a rest stop coming up. Let's just get the gas."

"So if I stop and get gas," he says, "you're going to stay with the car and not use the bathroom? Is that what you're telling me?"

"Well…" I can't lie and pretend I'm not going to use the bathroom. Because he will absolutely watch me and make sure I don't go. He will drive this point home, just out of spite. "I might use it if we stop."

"You are so full of shit, Claire."

Even though Rihanna is singing on the radio, the rest of the car is silent. Everyone is listening to this embarrassing argument. If we weren't traveling at seventy miles per hour, I would open the door and jump out of this car right now.

"Actually," Lindsay speaks up in a small voice, "I need to use the bathroom. Could we stop?"

At least Lindsay has my back. Noah glances over his shoulder, then grumbles, "Fine." Then he proceeds to cut across three lanes on the highway all at once, resulting in one near collision and a slew of angry horns. Apparently, Noah is trying to get us all killed during this trip.

I let Lindsay use the bathroom first, just to keep up the pretense of not actually needing the bathroom, even though I've got my legs crossed as I'm waiting outside the Porta-John behind the gas station. The whole time, I'm fuming at Noah. We're barely an hour into the drive, and he's already making things miserable for everyone. This was a mistake—I should never have agreed to this trip. But thank God we have separate rooms. Even though he seems angry about it, I've never been happier about that decision.

When I get out of the bathroom, Jack is waiting outside. He's typing something on his phone, and he brushes a strand of his shaggy dark hair out of his eyes. He's got a five-o'clock shadow, and it suits him—I always liked the way he looked with a little stubble. When he sees me, he lifts his puppy-dog brown eyes.

"Hey," he says.

"Hey," I say.

He shoves his phone into the pocket of his jeans. "Are you okay, Claire?"

I drop my eyes. "Yeah."

He glances around. The Porta-John is behind the gas station convenience store, hidden from the view of the gas pumps. My minivan is nowhere in sight. Everyone is probably back in the car by now. Or maybe buying snacks for the trip.

"He was being a real jerk to you," Jack says.

"Yeah," I agree. Even though Lindsay shot me a sympathetic look, it's good to hear somebody else say it out loud. Sometimes I wonder if I'm partially at fault for the way Noah behaves. But no. I didn't provoke what he did in the car. He was being a jerk to me for no reason.

"I'm sorry you have to deal with that," he says. "Noah didn't used to be like that. He's changed."

I nod. Jack knows my husband almost as well as I do. After all, they lived together before I lived with him. When we were in our twenties, Noah didn't have a friend closer than Jack. But in the last few years, they've grown apart. Hell, we've only had dinner with Jack and Michelle a dozen or so times since Emma was born.

"You don't deserve to be treated that way," he says.

My breath catches in my throat as he takes a step toward me. "Well, what can I do?"

He shakes his head. "I wish it could be different."

"Me too." My voice is shaking. "You have no idea."

He takes another step toward me, and this time, he lowers his lips onto mine. I melt into him, allowing him to press me against the jagged brick wall of the convenience store.

"Did you get the separate room?" he breathes in my ear.

"I sure did."

"Perfect." He grins at me, his eyes crinkling. "This is going to be a fantastic week. I'm going to make you forget all about him."

And even though everyone is waiting for us back at the car, I let him kiss me again.

CHAPTER 7

CLAIRE

Now you think I'm a terrible person.

I think I'm a terrible person too. What kind of decent human being does something like this? Not only am I cheating on my husband, but I'm doing it with his best friend. It's not just awful, it's cartoon villainy awful.

The best I could say is neither of us meant it to happen. It was just one of those things.

It all started back in February. Jack runs his own contracting business, and we were having our kitchen redone. Jack, being one of our oldest friends, gave us the friends-and-family price. He was supposed to be done by the time my school's winter break started, but he was still working by then. Both the kids were at a winter vacation camp, and I was stuck at home while the construction was ongoing.

I was just trying to be friendly—I swear. I would offer him some water or coffee. And then we would chat while he worked. I got to talking about me and Noah and about how things had gotten so bad lately. I'd always thought Jack and Michelle had a storybook marriage, but he revealed that wasn't the reality. He said she had become cold and distant lately, and she worked practically all the time. She made it very clear to him that work was her first priority. He was a distant second.

On the last day of winter break, Jack kissed me.

Nobody but Noah had touched me like that since I was twenty years old. And Noah himself hadn't touched me like that in a long time. I had started to think I was dead inside, but that kiss showed me I was wrong.

I wasn't dead. But Noah was killing me.

So for the last four months, we've been sneaking off together. Jack has flexible hours, so he can pop over at the end of the school day, when the kids are at their after-school activities. His house is always empty since Michelle barely leaves the office. They've made it almost too easy for us.

I'm falling in love with Jack. And I think he feels the same way about me. But there's nothing we can do about it. If I left Noah under these circumstances, it would be a horrible, messy divorce. I don't want to do that to the kids. And if Jack left his divorce-lawyer wife under *any* circumstances, she would destroy him.

So we live for these little moments we have together. And we know it can't go on forever, so we're just trying to enjoy it while it lasts.

I allow Jack to kiss me for about fifteen seconds, then I gently push him away. "We have to get back to the car."

"Yeah." He lifts an eyebrow suggestively. "I can't wait to get you alone."

"Me too." A fantasy fills my head. What if Jack and I grabbed an Uber and just took off together right now and didn't look back? Well, I'd obviously come back to get my kids, but we could at least disappear for the week. I would give anything to get out of this toxic car ride. But obviously, that's not possible. "We better go."

I go out first so it doesn't look suspicious. Noah is standing beside the minivan, and he looks up sharply when he sees me. He has an unreadable expression on his face, and for a moment, my stomach turns to ice. Does he suspect?

I don't want Noah to know. It's entirely possible he's cheating on me too, and that idea doesn't even bother me. But the fact that this is happening with Jack... That's the part I think would kill him. His best friend. One of his *only* friends. Men have been driven to the brink over lesser betrayals.

"You done using the bathroom?" he asks.

"You done getting gas?" I retort.

"Yep."

Jack emerges from the back of the convenience store, whistling a little tune to himself. It's time to get back on the road. I brace myself and climb inside.

The car is stifling. I slide the window open, and I want to stick out my face. It's only the end of June, but it's really hot today. If it doesn't cool down, we're not going to be able to do much outdoors during this trip.

"Close the window," Noah says.

"It's stuffy in here."

"I turned on the air conditioner."

"Well, I don't feel it yet. When it starts up, I'll close the window."

"The car is never going to get cool if you've got the window wide open. I'm not sure why I need to explain that to you."

I feel a lump in my throat. I don't think I realized quite how bad things were between me and Noah until this trip. I want to reach out with my bare hands and strangle him right now.

"Hey, listen." Warner's baritone interrupts my murderous thoughts. "I just wanted to let you know I printed out some paper maps to help us find the place."

Lindsay beams at him. "You're always so prepared!"

Noah glances over his shoulder, then taps the navigation screen on the dashboard of the minivan. "No need. I plugged it into the GPS."

"Yeah, but we might lose the signal when we get closer. It's sort of in the middle of nowhere."

For the first time during this trip, Noah looks uncomfortable. I remember from back in our college days, before we had GPS navigation, how frustrated he would get if we ever got lost. "You think we're going to lose our signal?" he asks.

"I need to be able to access the internet!" Michelle speaks up. She sounds slightly hysterical. "I've got a lot of work to do! I can't be cut off from the world."

"The inn has Wi-Fi," Warner assures her, never losing composure in his perfect features. "But around that area, the signal is spotty. I just thought it was safer to print out some maps."

"It'll be fine, Noah," Jack says. "I'm great at map navigation. I've even got a compass in my bag. It's one of the things I learned when I was—"

"A Boy Scout," Noah finishes. "Right. I remember."

Warner's prediction about losing our internet signal makes me anxious though. I don't want to lose access to my phone. What if Penny calls about the kids? Emma is already not coping well, and I hate the idea of her not being able to reach us. I quickly shoot off a text to Penny:

> Just a heads up we may lose phone access when we get close to the hotel. Will call you tonight.

I take a deep breath and try to relax. There's nothing we can do. It won't be long before we're at the inn. I just have to hang in there.

CHAPTER 8

CLAIRE

At around the two-hour mark, we see a sign for a rest stop that contains a McDonald's and a small diner. I'm in the mood for some greasy french fries, but I get over-ruled and we end up at the diner. I'm still going to get some greasy fries. It's the only way I can make it through the rest of this drive.

The diner is surprisingly busy for a rest-stop location. The walls are lined with booths, with larger tables in the middle, and ironic street signs litter the walls. The entire place smells like grease and burgers. I inhale deeply, already decided I'm going to get a big juicy burger.

While the others are being led to a table, Lindsay and I go to the bathroom together to wash our hands. That's what we say anyway, and I actually do wash my hands, since the last thing I touched was that Porta-John. But Lindsay seems to be more interested in fixing her makeup. She stares critically at her face in the bathroom mirror, which is at least twice as pretty as mine—much more if you take into account the circles under my eyes from Emma tossing and turning in our bed all week. I can't imagine what Lindsay is seeing in the mirror that she doesn't like.

She pulls out a tube of pink lipstick and applies a fresh layer to her lips. She smiles at me in the mirror. "So what do you think of Warner?"

"I've only known him for a couple of hours," I point out. We've barely exchanged any words—it's far too soon to form an opinion. "But he seems...nice."

"He's cute, isn't he?" she says.

"Definitely." Warner is far more than "cute." *Noah* is cute. Warner is drop-dead gorgeous. Even if I were single, I could never get a guy who looked like him. I wouldn't even want to. Everybody would just look at the two of us and wonder what the hell he was doing with *me*.

"Listen..." Lindsay places the cap back on her lipstick and turns to me. She lowers her voice a notch. "There's something I should tell you."

I raise my eyebrows. "Yes?"

Lindsay opens her mouth, but before she can say anything, the door to the ladies' room swings open. It's Michelle.

Michelle takes a step back, her fingers lingering on the door, as if she's not sure if she should turn around and leave. I sort of wish she would, because I'm dying to know what Lindsay has to tell me. But we can't talk in front of Michelle.

When Jack and Michelle were first dating, Lindsay and I made an effort to be friendly with her. The three of us went out to dinner a couple of times, but it was obvious we just didn't click. I also didn't like how Michelle *always* found fault in her meal and sent it back. Doesn't she know people spit in your food if you do that?

Still, because Jack and Noah were such good friends, I kept trying to make an effort to invite her out. I figured if we spent enough time together, we would get to be friends. Jack liked her, after all. But after we went out twice, she always seems to have an excuse for why she couldn't go. When I gently asked Jack about it once, he mumbled something about how she was busy with work. I got the hint.

And of course, now that I'm sleeping with her husband, it's hardly the time for us to start bonding.

Michelle's sharp eyes dart between the two of us. Even in her blue jeans and fitted white T-shirt, she looks like she could be on her way to the office. I don't know how she manages to always look so put together. She's about five years older than us—she had already finished law school and was practicing when she and Jack started dating—but she has the kind of classic looks that make it hard to tell her age. She'll be as attractive at fifty as she was at twenty-five.

"Excuse me," she says to us as she moves toward the empty sink.

The three of us stand in awkward silence while Michelle lathers up her hands, then rinses them off. She's doing quite a thorough job cleaning them. I wonder if she sings the happy birthday song in her head while she does it, like we teach the kids in school. Probably not.

"It's good to be out of the car, isn't it?" I say, just to break the silence.

Michelle lifts her eyes to look at me, but she doesn't say anything. For a split second, I wonder if she might know the truth.

But no. She doesn't know. Jack and I were careful.

"I love your earrings," Lindsay says.

Michelle's fingers fly to her right ear. Her cheeks are pink with pride—Lindsay is amazing at knowing exactly what to compliment someone on. "Thank you. They were my mother's."

We wait for a beat, to see if Michelle will offer a compliment to either of us. She doesn't. Just as well, because it wouldn't be sincere.

When we get back out to the restaurant, the boys are seated at a six-person rectangular table. Noah and Warner are on one side, with an empty seat between them, which Lindsay quickly grabs. Jack is on the other side, in the center. Michelle sits on one side of him, and I sit on the other. Of the three couples, Noah and I are the only ones not sitting together. Which is fine by me, because I don't want to be anywhere near him right now.

"Everything on the menu looks so good," Jack says. His sneaker rubs against mine as he flashes me a quick, meaningful look. Are we really going to risk playing footsie under the table? I guess we are.

As she examines the menu, Lindsay plays with a strand of blond hair that came loose from her bun. Lindsay has the best hair of anyone I know. She always has. It's ash blond, perfectly highlighted, and silky soft. After college, she tried her hand at advertising and finance, but she ultimately decided to become a hairdresser. She's great at it.

"I love the burgers at these little diners." Lindsay inhales deeply. "You can smell them cooking."

"I know!" I say. "They're always so juicy and fresh."

Warner frowns. "You're not going to get a burger, are you, Lindsay? Those things have, like, a thousand calories."

For the first time since I met Lindsay's Adonis of a boyfriend, I feel a trace of misgivings. Is he really trying to control what she eats? I attempt to catch Lindsay's eye, but she's looking down at the menu.

"Lindsay and I are training to run a marathon next month," Warner explains. "We need to keep in good shape."

"A marathon?" My mouth falls open. "Lindsay, *you're* going to run a marathon?"

She smiles, but it looks forced. "Oh, yes! We're so excited!"

Warner throws his arm around her narrow shoulders. "Lindsay is doing great with her training. She's a powerhouse!"

This isn't like my best friend at all. Lindsay does Pilates, not marathons. She hates working up a sweat. And anyway, she doesn't need to watch what she eats. She's in great shape.

I get the greasy burger with french fries, and the best I can say is that there's no negative commentary from Noah. He gets a burger too: "Rare. Bloody. Maybe still mooing." Warner orders a turkey sandwich—no mayo. (At least he isn't a hypocrite.) And Lindsay gets a side salad—no dressing.

Right after we place our orders, Michelle looks down at her watch. Every time I've seen her, she always seems to be in a hurry. But I swear she's looked at her watch three times since we walked in here.

"Are things busy at work, Michelle?" I ask politely.

She smiles tightly. "Always. But yeah, it's been very busy lately." She laughs. "People really hate their spouses."

"What do you do, Michelle?" Warner asks.

She toys with the napkin in front of her. "I'm a divorce attorney."

"Oh?" Warner's lips twitch. "You must see some brutal stuff."

A smile touches her lips. "Are you divorced?"

It's sort of a personal question for somebody she just met an hour ago, but Michelle is used to being blunt. Anyway, Warner doesn't seem bothered. "No," he says. "When I get married, it will be forever."

And Lindsay beams. God, she's gaga for this guy.

"Nice sentiment. For your sake, I hope you're right." Michelle shakes her head. "Unfortunately, most people aren't so lucky."

I avoid looking at Noah. I don't want to admit that Michelle's statement has touched a nerve.

"I have this one client…" She pauses, uncertain if she should go on. "It's a bit of a long story."

"Tell us!" Lindsay demands. She puts her hand on Warner's golden-haired forearm. "Michelle tells the *best* stories."

Michelle smiles at another of Lindsay's well-placed compliments, although she knows it's true. "This one is a doozy. My client was married to this rich banker. He cheated on her multiple times, and we were going to take him to the cleaners. Like, the guy was going to be living in his *car* after this."

Jack and I exchange quick glances. There's no doubt in his mind that if he ever decided to leave Michelle, he'd be lucky if he even got to keep his car. He'd be living in a cardboard box. And not a nice cardboard box either.

"Anyway," Michelle says, "the guy was desperate. So…"

I suck in a breath. "So…?"

"He hired a hit man to knock her off."

We're all wearing identical expressions of shock. Nothing like that ever happens at the school where I work. It's an exciting day when somebody gets pinched really hard.

"Unfortunately for him," Michelle says, "a neighbor was able to get the license plate on the hit man's car. The police caught up with him, and in exchange for immunity, he turned the husband in. Now, instead of living in his car, the husband is going to be living in a jail cell for the rest of his life."

Jack has turned two shades paler. The truth is he's wanted to leave Michelle for years. He realized a long time ago they weren't right for each other. And he had always been hoping she would change her mind about not wanting any kids, but she's made it clear that's not going to happen.

But what can he do? Best-case scenario, Michelle would destroy him.

And what if she finds out the two of us are having an affair? What will she do then?

"What sort of work do you do, Warner?" Michelle asks.

"Plastic surgeon," he says.

Michelle snaps her fingers. "That's what my client's husband did. He was a plastic surgeon too."

Warner tugs at the collar of his shirt. "Interesting coincidence. What's his name?"

She winks at him. "I can't share that information, unfortunately. Where do you work?"

"St. Mary's."

Jack leans forward and his knee brushes against mine.

"St. Mary's… Hey, my friend Buddy Levine is the medical director there. You must know Buddy."

Warner nods vigorously. "Of course I do. Good man."

"Say hi for me when you get back to work, will you?"

Warner smiles. "Will do, Jack."

When he smiles like that, he's so handsome you almost have to look away. Lindsay is almost slobbering over him, which unsettles me. I've never seen her so infatuated—she's usually fairly cool around the opposite sex—and I'm not convinced it's a good thing.

Warner turns his vivid blue eyes in my direction. "Lindsay tells me you're a teacher, Claire."

Despite my reservations, I have to smile. I'm pleased Lindsay was talking to her new boyfriend about my work, and I'm even more pleased he's considerate enough to remember details about her friends. This is a clear point in Warner's favor.

"That's right," I say. "I teach special ed."

Warner takes a swig from his water glass. "I really admire people like you. Honestly. I could never be a teacher."

"Oh?" I say.

"The salary is…" He shakes his head. "For such an important job, it's a crime how badly they pay you guys."

"Well…" I feel my smile falter—he's not wrong. "It would be nice if they paid us what we deserve."

"And it's so *repetitive*." He shudders. "I think you teachers deserve an award for what they put you through. Really—bravo, Claire."

I take a moment to absorb his words. He's paying me a compliment, so I suppose I should be flattered. But I don't appreciate being told how much my job sucks. Especially because I do love it so much. "It can be a little repetitive at times," I admit. "But it's really rewarding. And every job eventually gets to be repetitive after a number of years."

He nods thoughtfully. "Yes, that's true. I feel rather fortunate to be in a field that never gets repetitive."

I raise an eyebrow. "You mean you don't get sick of doing boob jobs after a while?"

He flashes his straight, white teeth at me. I hope he had braces when he was a kid, or else life really isn't fair. "I *definitely* never get sick of doing boob jobs. I could do them all day long." He tightens his grip around Lindsay's shoulders. "You hear that, Lindsay?"

I flinch. Is he suggesting *Lindsay* needs a boob job? She absolutely does not. I wait for Lindsay to roll her eyes or elbow him in the chest, but she doesn't. Her cheeks grow pink, and she folds her arms self-consciously across her chest.

This guy might be great looking, but I'm beginning to wonder if Lindsay is trying to be someone she's not just to impress him.

When the food arrives, I pick up my burger and start eating practically before my plate touches the table. There's something about long car rides that makes you desperately hungry. I glance at Lindsay with her sad little side salad. We *really* need to have a talk later. I know she says she likes Warner, but I have to dig deeper. We can go on a hike together and she'll tell me the whole story.

I wonder what she wanted to tell me in the bathroom before Michelle interrupted us.

"Excuse me, miss," Michelle speaks up as the waitress is getting ready to walk away.

The waitress brushes a stray strand of hair from her face and flashes Michelle a tired smile. "Yes, hon?"

Michelle pushes her plate away from her with the tip of her index finger. "I asked for my burger to be medium well, but this is really more medium. And the fries are burned."

I look over at Michelle's fries. They don't look burned to me. Maybe a little crispy, but still delicious.

"I'm so sorry," the waitress says quickly. She takes Michelle's plate. "I'll get you some new food right away."

Jack rolls his eyes at me so quickly I'm sure nobody else at the table sees it. He can't stand it when Michelle sends back her food. *Can't we have one damn meal where she doesn't find fault in her order?*

My phone buzzes with a text. I pull it out of my purse and see a message from Penny:

Emma settled down. I've got everybody watching cartoons, and I'm making mac and cheese for lunch.

I smile at the text. Emma's favorite food is macaroni and cheese. She would probably eat it for every meal, including breakfast, if I let her.

"Emma's okay," I tell Noah.

He grunts with a mouth full of burger.

"What's wrong with Emma?" Lindsay asks. She's Emma's godmother, and the kids think of her as family.

"She had this dream that a monster was going to eat us," I say.

Lindsay clasps a hand over her mouth. "Oh no! Poor thing."

"It's Claire's fault," Noah announces to the table. "She fills her head with nonsense, and this is what happens."

My mouth falls open. "It's *my* fault? I filled her head with *nonsense*?"

Noah puts down his half-eaten burger and glares at me across the table. "You're not honest with them. I mean, if you tell them the tooth fairy is real, why shouldn't they believe in monsters?"

This is an argument Noah and I have had many times before. He feels strongly that the tooth fairy, the Easter bunny, and even Santa are not things parents should ever lie to their kids about. But I hate the idea of my kids being the only ones at school who never believed in the magic of Santa. I remember the first time Aidan lost a baby tooth and I told him the tooth fairy was going to put something special under his pillow, and he said, "I know it's just you." It was a jab in my heart.

Aidan has always been more practical, like his father, but Emma is different. Even though Noah has assured her that all these things aren't real, she still secretly believes Santa comes down our chimney on Christmas Eve. I love that about her.

"There's nothing wrong with pretending the tooth fairy is real," I say. "It doesn't hurt them."

"Obviously it does." Noah's eyes are flashing, even through his glasses. "Because now she thinks a monster is going to eat us."

I appeal to the rest of the table. "I don't think there's anything horrible about a kid believing in Santa. Is there?"

"I loved waiting for Santa on Christmas Eve when I was a kid," Lindsay sighs. I can always count on her to stick up for me. "I looked forward to it all year."

"But it's all a *lie*." Noah frowns. "I'm sorry, but I can't outright lie to my children. They deserve to know the truth."

"It's all just in fun," Warner says. "I don't see anything wrong with it."

Noah blinks at us. "So nobody has a problem with making kids believe that a morbidly obese man comes down the chimney with a giant bag of presents? Nobody else is troubled by that?"

"Geez, Noah," Jack says. "When did you get to be such a Grinch?"

I would have thought Noah would sit here arguing about the evils of Santa Claus for the next hour, but when Jack says that, he jerks his head back like he got punched. He stands up abruptly from the table, leaving his half-eaten plate of food. He reaches into his wallet, pulls out a couple of twenties, and drops them on the table.

"I'm done eating. I'm going to wait in the car," he says.

As Noah storms out of the diner, I feel Jack's hand under the table take my own. He gives me a squeeze with his big, warm palm. But it doesn't make me feel even a tiny bit better.

"I...I think I'm going to go get some air," I gulp.

I rise unsteadily to my feet and stumble out of the diner. I see Noah over by the minivan, so I go in the opposite direction. There's a little nook behind the diner that's quiet and isolated. And it only smells slightly like garbage.

I take a shaky breath. My eyes are watery and I swipe at them with the back of my hand. I don't want to cry right now, because my eyes will get all red and puffy, and when I get back to the car, everyone will know. I've got to keep it together.

Keep it together, Claire. Only a couple more hours and you don't have to see him again for the rest of the trip.

I don't know what to do anymore. I had thought I could stay with Noah long enough to get through the kids at least being in high school, but I don't know if that's possible anymore. This trip has opened up my eyes. We hate each other.

God, I don't know what to do.

"Claire?"

Lindsay is standing behind me, her pink lips pursed. I had thought Jack might be the one to come check on me, but of course he couldn't. Not with Michelle sitting right there.

"Hey," I say.

She chews on her lip. "Are you okay?"

I nod, even though I'm not actually okay. "Yeah. I just needed some air."

Lindsay opens her mouth, but she doesn't look quite certain what she wants to say. She's been around since Noah and I first started dating. She used to do my hair with the curling iron before he and I would go out. I've confided in her some of the problems I've had with Noah, but I've played it down. I don't want to bore her with all my married-life problems. She doesn't want to hear about our millionth argument over the toilet paper.

But when she finally does speak, what she says surprises me: "I saw you and Jack at the gas station."

My heart skips in my chest. Is she saying what I think she's saying? Maybe not. I'm going to play dumb. "What... what do you mean?"

Her face falls. "You know what I mean. I saw the two of you...you know, *kissing*. I was going to tell you in the bathroom, but then Michelle walked in and..."

"Oh." I drop my eyes and kick at the ground with my sneaker. "I see."

"Claire…"

"Don't say it." My eyes fill with fresh tears. "You see the way he treats me."

"I know." She steps closer, and I can feel her soft hand rest on my shoulder. "I don't blame you, honestly. He's horrible to you. But to do it with *Jack*… I mean, he's—"

"He's Noah's best friend. I *know*."

Lindsay throws her arms around me, enveloping me in a hug. And that pretty much does it—I start sobbing. I'm getting tears and snot all over Lindsay's tank top, but she seems okay with it. It makes me realize how long it's been since I've had a really good hug.

We stand there for way too long before I finally pull away. I can tell without looking in a mirror that my eyes are swollen. "I'm sorry," I say.

"For what?"

I shake my head. "I'm a terrible person."

"You're not a terrible person." Lindsay brushes a wet strand of hair from my face. "But if you want to leave Noah, you should leave him. Don't mess around behind his back."

"You're right." I accept the crumpled tissue Lindsay hands me. "I really don't want him to find out about me and Jack."

She tilts her head to the side. "You don't think he already knows?"

My heart sinks into my stomach. "You…you think he knows?"

"Well…" She shifts her weight between her boots. "Yes. I do. I think he knows."

"Why?"

"It's just a feeling I get." She cranes her head to look over at the minivan. Noah is sitting inside, in the driver's seat. He's just staring straight out the windshield, unmoving. "I mean, I've known Noah for fifteen years, and I've never seen him act this way before. He's generally pretty even-tempered."

"Yeah."

She's right. Noah has recently stepped up his game when it comes to being obnoxious to me. Things had been getting gradually worse for so long, I just thought it was part of the trajectory. But maybe there's a reason things have gotten so much worse lately. Maybe he *does* know.

Once again, I get that strong feeling I should back out of the trip now, while I still have a chance. As much as I'm looking forward to having a room alone with Jack, it isn't worth the risk. Michelle could find out. Noah could find out, if he doesn't know already. And this trip seems to be putting the final nail in the coffin when it comes to our marriage.

But I don't know how I'm going to get home at this point. We've been driving for two hours, so it wouldn't be a quick ride back home. It would cost a fortune.

It looks like I'm stuck. This trip is happening. But I'm going to take Lindsay's advice. As soon as we get back to Castle Pines, I'm telling Noah it's over.

CHAPTER 9

CLAIRE

It takes all my willpower to march back to my minivan and sit down next to Noah in the passenger seat. The others have already taken their seats in the back, and I'm tempted to ask one of them if they'd like to trade. I don't want to sit next to Noah. But it would be awkward to say that, so I sit down. And he shoots me a look like he wishes he had taken off without me.

Sometimes I look back on my marriage and try to figure out the exact moment when Noah and I started hating each other.

Like I said, we loved each other when we got married. We were one of those couples that never even fought. Like, we would have minor, stupid arguments about…I don't know, maybe I turned up the heat too high in the winter. Or I caught him drinking out of the milk carton. (Why do men do that?) But it was usually stuff we would laugh about—teasing more than fighting. We were both easygoing people who hated to fight, and sometimes

Noah would mumble something about "not wanting to end up like my parents."

After Aidan was born, life got harder. We were excited to be parents but also scared. Noah would sometimes sit bolt upright in the middle of the night and not be able to get back to sleep until he went to Aidan's crib to make sure he was still present and breathing. Other times, we would have serious arguments about whose turn it was to change his diaper. Noah created a sign-in sheet on the refrigerator to keep track, but he took it down when he realized how far behind he was getting.

But still, I always thought we had a happy little family. Then Emma came along.

Emma is wonderful. Don't get me wrong—I love my daughter more than life itself and I'd do anything for her. But she was not an easy baby. She had colic, and all she did was scream. I mean, I suppose she also occasionally slept and ate, but it felt like 99 percent of the time, she was screaming. When I look back on that time, all I remember is this little pink baby with her eyes squeezed shut, her hands balled into fists, and her toothless mouth wide open as she hollered at the top of her lungs. And we also had a toddler to contend with. The first few months of Emma's life felt like a haze of the two of us passing her back and forth, stealing an hour or two of sleep whenever we could.

It was doable when I was on maternity leave. But then the summer ended and I had to go back to work. Emma was sleeping a little better by then, but not much. Noah and I were sleeping in shifts. It was awful.

On one particular night, I was determined to get a half-decent night of sleep because I had a big meeting at work the next morning where I was talking to the school board about the special education program at our school. It was a really, really important meeting, and I didn't think I could get through it on an hour of sleep. I pumped Emma full of two bottles of milk, hoping she'd conk out but knowing it was a crapshoot.

I told Noah about the meeting and emphasized how important it was. I *had* to get a decent night of sleep. He swore he understood. So when Emma woke up screaming at two in the morning, I expected him to get up with her.

"I've got a headache, Claire," he mumbled into his pillow. "Can't you get her?"

I had a headache too. I had a headache almost all the time those days as well as big purple circles under my eyes. Skipping out on my parental duties was never an option. "You know I have a big meeting tomorrow."

Noah squeezed his eyes shut. After a long minute of Emma's cries increasing in volume, he got out of bed and slammed the door shut behind him when he left the bedroom.

Just as the cries subsided and I started to drift off again, the screams abruptly started again. A few seconds later, Noah came back into the bedroom. He flopped down on the bed and covered his head with the pillow.

"I can't deal with her," he said. "You have to do it."

"But I told you, I have a meeting tomorrow!"

"Well, I have a headache. I'm not getting up."

And that was it as far as he was concerned. He acted like Emma was *my* baby, he was doing me a *favor* by trying to help, but if he didn't want to do it, he didn't have to. I remember staring at him in the dark bedroom, waiting to see if he would change his mind. He didn't budge. I had to get up and spend the rest of the night comforting Emma.

He never apologized for that one. Even though I was a wreck at my meeting the next day, and he ended up sleeping in after I dropped Emma and Aidan off at day care. It was so incredibly unfair.

After that, it seemed like we were at war more and more frequently. He never carried his weight when it came to the children and the housework, and what's worse, he didn't *care*. He told me all I did was nag him. We stopped doing things together as a family—I preferred to go out with the kids myself so I didn't have to watch him play with his phone instead of talking to me. And we never did anything together as a couple. I can't remember our last date night. For a while, we were making an effort to get a babysitter and go out, but I can't remember the last time either of us even suggested it.

I kept telling myself things would get better as the kids got older. But now they're older. And it turned out our marriage got too broken to fix.

And now we're stuck together in this car. For *hours*. It's become the most awkward car ride in the history of the world. I would give anything to get out of it. Occasionally, I hear some conversation from the back, but for the most part, we are all deathly silent. I am having trouble envisioning anything I could say that won't result in a fight between me and Noah, and I don't want to have another fight with him in front of everyone.

At this point, I just want to get the week over with so I can tell him it's over. Hopefully, he won't hire a hit man to take me out, but it wouldn't entirely surprise me.

For the last half hour, the road we're on has become progressively more narrow and isolated. I don't think we've seen another car in twenty minutes. The pavement here is cracked and unkempt. My minivan's tires snap fallen branches in the road and lurch on the uneven ground.

"Turn left onto Appleton Road," the GPS voice instructs us.

Noah hits the brakes just as we come across the sign for Appleton Road. It's a tiny road that goes one way. The pavement has been uneven up until now, but this road is entirely unpaved. Noah hesitates with his foot on the brake.

"This is the turn here," Warner speaks up.

"Right." Noah taps his fingers against the wheel. He's anxious about going down this road. Unlike Jack, he's no former Boy Scout. We've never been camping together in all our years of marriage. "Okay."

Noah turns down Appleton Road, and immediately the ride gets a lot rougher. There are no other cars around—it's just us and the wilderness. I hold on to my seat as we make our way down this uneven path. But we're close now. It's not too much farther to the inn.

And then the picture on the GPS freezes.

Noah keeps his eyes on the road as he taps the screen. Up on top, the words appear: *Searching for signal…*

"Damn," he mutters under his breath.

"I've got the map," Warner speaks up.

I hear him shuffling through his duffel bag. I pull my phone out of my purse—there's no signal there either. I feel about as uneasy as Noah looks. I'm not any more comfortable with the wilderness than he is. I can't wait to get to the inn and have Wi-Fi access.

I wish I had called the kids back when we were on the main road. I had been thinking I would call them when we got to the inn, but now I wish I hadn't waited. Even though I gave Penny a heads-up, I imagine Emma being worried.

"All right," Warner says, "there's going to be a fork in the road coming up, and you need to go left."

"Right," Noah says.

"No, he said left," I say.

"I *know* he said left," Noah snaps at me. "I was saying 'right,' like I got it."

I swallow hard. "Okay. I was just making sure. I didn't mean to..."

"Could you just... Just don't talk to me, Claire. I need to focus."

Noah presses his fingers against his eyeballs under his glasses, then focuses his attention back on the road. We come to the fork, and he slows to a complete halt. The road diverges in two directions, but the right path seems much better paved. The left is more narrow and has branches hanging down everywhere. The sun is still in the sky, but the left path looks dark and foreboding. If there's a monster out here in the woods, it's definitely on the left.

"Are you sure we're supposed to go left?" Noah asks.

Warner looks up from the map. "Two roads diverged in a yellow wood," he recites in that rich baritone. "And I took the one less traveled by, and that has made all the difference."

Noah crinkles his nose. "What the..." he mutters under his breath.

I clasp my hand over my mouth to suppress a giggle, and for a split second, Noah looks proud of himself for making me laugh. For that half a second, it's almost like the old days again, before we hated each other. When we could share an emotion without even having to exchange words.

"Warner is quoting that poem," Lindsay says. "You

know. The one by Robert Frost?" She shoots her boy-friend a loving look. "He's *very* well read."

"Yes, I know it," Noah says tightly. "But what the hell does that have to do with how to get to the inn?"

"You take the path on the left," Warner explains. "It may be less traveled, but it's the correct path."

Noah doesn't look at all thrilled about it, but he takes Robert Frost's advice and turns left at the fork. It isn't even a road anymore. It's a dirt path. It's very hard to imagine that a reputable establishment wouldn't have a decent road to get there. I mean, what's next? Are we going to have to drive across some rickety drawbridge?

After another twenty minutes of driving very slowly, Noah comes to a complete halt. He looks over his shoulder at Warner. "There's no way this is right."

Warner fumbles with the map in his hand. "No, we're on target. It's another two miles and we're there."

Noah throws the car into park. "Let me see the map."

Warner hands it over. I look over Noah's shoulder—the map is not that easy to read. It's printed out on an eight-by-eleven-inch sheet of white paper, and everything is super tiny. Noah turns it ninety degrees, squinting down at the minuscule print.

"Do you want me to take a look at it, Noah?" Jack calls from the back row.

"I'm the one driving, so no." Noah clears his throat. "Okay. I think I see where to go."

He shifts the car back into drive, but the engine is strangely silent. Noah frowns as he presses his foot onto the gas. What now?

"The car stalled." He looks at me. "Does your car do this a lot?"

I bite my lip. "No. Never."

"When is the last time you got it serviced?"

"I don't know. Six months ago?"

"You don't *know*?" he repeats.

"I said about six months ago. Give or take." I think it was six months ago. I remember taking it to the mechanic right after a particularly brutal fight about why there was no fresh milk in the house. There was snow on the ground, so it was sometime during the winter.

Noah kills the engine, then tries to restart the car. I hear a clicking noise, but the engine doesn't catch. He tries again with the same result.

"The battery is dead." He blinks down at the dash-board. "The car won't start."

"I've got jumper cables in the back," I say.

He snorts. "Great. Do you also have a battery in the back that we can give it a jump off of?"

Oh. I guess he has a point.

He unbuckles his seat belt. "Let me take a look under the hood."

"Take a look?" I repeat. Noah may be a physicist, but he doesn't know anything about cars. "What do you think you're going to see under there? An on/off switch on the battery that's toggled to off?"

I probably shouldn't have said that. It was sort of mean. On the other hand, the idea of Noah looking under the hood and discovering something wrong with the car that can be fixed right here and now seems just short of impossible.

Noah shoots me a dirty look as he pops the hood and climbs out of the car. Jack and Warner get out too, and the three men huddle together under the hood, debating what could have caused my relatively new minivan to suddenly stop working in the middle of nowhere. I watch Noah's face as he talks to Jack. The two of them have been friends for almost two decades. Does Noah know about me and Jack?

I can't tell.

"I'm sure they'll fix the problem," Lindsay says confidently.

"I don't know," I mumble. I wish I had her optimism. Noah and Jack don't know cars. It's possible Warner is a car expert, but he doesn't look like it, if I'm being honest.

What are we going to do if we don't get the car running? We're nowhere near the main road. And none of us have cell reception.

Noah slams the hood closed again and gets back in the driver's seat. I can tell from his face he's not optimistic. He turns the key in the ignition, and there's only that clicking noise again. He drops his head against the headrest. "Great." He cranes his head to look at everyone in the back. "Does anyone have a signal on their phone?"

The panic is starting to mount in my chest. I pull my phone out of my purse again with trembling hands—no signal. The negative responses echo from the back of the vehicle. None of us has a signal. We're stuck out here, and there's no way to call for help.

"Listen, don't panic." Warner shakes the map in his hand. "Like I said, we're only two miles away from the inn. We can walk there, and then we'll send somebody to get the car."

"Walk there?" Lindsay doesn't sound thrilled about that idea. She's not exactly outdoorsy either. "I thought if you get lost in the woods, you're supposed to stay put."

"Under some circumstances," Warner says and nods. "But nobody is going to be looking for us in the near future. We're not expected back home for a week. And we've got a map showing us exactly where to go. It would be stupid not to try to find this place."

Lindsay frowns. "Yes, but…"

"Trust me on this, Lindsay." Warner pats her shoulder. "You just don't know better."

I don't like the patronizing way Warner is speaking to her. Ever since he kept her from getting the burger she wanted at the diner, this guy has been getting on my nerves. Once I get her alone, I'm going to have a talk with her about him.

"I can't sit in this car waiting for somebody to rescue us for several days," Michelle says firmly. "I've got a lot of work to do, people."

Yes, we know.

"Also," Warner adds, "we don't have much food. Or water."

That last comment makes my heart skip a beat. He's right. Aside from maybe a bag of chips or some beef jerky bought at the convenience store, we don't have any food. Noah's got a half-full water bottle in the cupholder, but that's about it. The six of us aren't going to be able to survive here for several days if we stay put.

My stomach lets out a low growl. I only ate about a third of the burger at the diner. I lost my appetite after Noah stormed out. Now I wish I had finished it.

"I've got my compass," Jack volunteers. "It shouldn't be difficult to navigate there."

Lindsay shakes her head and hugs her chest. "I don't know. I really think we should stay put."

"*You* can stay in the car if you'd like," Warner tells her. There's a bit of an edge to his voice that I hadn't heard before.

Her blue eyes dart around the car. She leans forward in my direction. "Claire, are you going to go?"

"I don't know."

She grabs my wrist with her long, skinny fingers. "Let's stay in the car. It's safer here."

I look out the window of the minivan. The path ahead of us is littered with branches and rocks and God knows what else. Why oh why did we have to take the road less traveled? What a mistake. Stupid Robert Frost.

But I don't want to be left behind in the car. What if everyone else reaches the inn and they can't find the car again? I don't want to be stuck here. If Lindsay and I stay behind, we have no chance of finding our way there. Neither of us has the slightest clue how to navigate through the wilderness. Warner has the only map, but even if I had a copy of that confusing guide to the inn, I doubt I'd be able to follow it.

And we have almost no food or water.

"I think we should stay together," I decide.

Lindsay frowns. "Are you sure?"

I nod, even though I'm far from sure. But it seems like the better of two bad options. Jack will make sure nothing happens to us.

"Okay," Lindsay says, but she doesn't sound thrilled.

Warner swings his arm around her shoulders. "Don't worry, babe. We know what we're doing. It's only two miles."

Two miles. It's two miles from our house to the children's school. When I walk it, it takes me about forty minutes. But it's got to take longer to walk through the forest. It'll probably take two hours. So in two hours, we'll be at the inn. I'll be able to kick off my shoes and take a long, hot bath in my private bathroom. I can't wait.

For the most part, we leave all our bags in the minivan. It's going to be hard enough to get through the woods without carrying a bunch of junk. I bring my purse, and Noah gives me his water bottle to put inside, which I nestle next to my phone. On the off chance we get a signal somewhere, I want to be prepared. Also, I want to make sure to send Penny a text the second we get there so that the kids know we're okay—especially Emma. Jack brings a backpack with supplies he brought for hiking, including a large water bottle that's nearly full. He stuffs his compass into his jeans pocket.

It's hot outside the car. Sweltering. Before the battery went out, the temperature gauge from outside the vehicle read eighty-nine degrees. We haven't even started walking yet, and I already feel hot and sticky. While I feel lucky to be the only one wearing shorts, my bare legs are too exposed. What if I step in poison ivy? What if a snake bites my ankle? I sort of wish I were wearing jeans instead, but my luggage is at the bottom of the pile, and I don't want to go through the hassle of changing inside the minivan. The shorts will be fine for a quick hike.

The dirt road disappears rapidly and is barely a road anymore—I can't imagine how the minivan would have made it any farther, even if the battery hadn't died. But the men seem confident as they lead the way. Jack has his compass and his Boy Scout experience, and Warner has the map and is the only one who has been here before. The three of us women bring up the rear.

"I'm sure it won't be too far," I say. I'm not by any means sure of that, but I'm trying to be optimistic for Lindsay's sake.

Michelle shoots me a look. "Don't you ever service your car, Claire?"

I flinch. "Yes. I service it regularly."

"Well, it seems to me," she says, "if you were going to take your vehicle on a trip out into the wilderness, you might want to bring it to the mechanic first to make sure it doesn't break down in the middle of nowhere."

I already got yelled at by Noah. I'm not in the mood to take it from Michelle too. But at the same time, I'm reluctant to get into a fight with her. I'm afraid of what might come out. "The minivan is new. There's no reason it should have broken down."

"Yet it did."

I take a deep, calming breath. "Look, we'll be there soon. This isn't that big a deal."

Michelle shakes her head at me, then without another word, she picks up her speed until she catches up with the men, leaving Lindsay and me behind.

"That was rude," I mumble.

Lindsay watches Michelle in the distance. "Maybe she knows."

"She doesn't know."

"I don't know. She seems even more ornery than usual."

"Yeah." I squint at Michelle's backside. She's in pretty good shape considering she spends her days behind a desk. I wonder if she works out. "But I think if she knew, she'd say something. She wouldn't just keep it to herself. That's not her style."

"Maybe." Lindsay cocks her head to the side. "But maybe she wouldn't say anything. I mean, it's not like either of us knows Michelle very well."

She has a point. Despite all our efforts, neither of us knows Michelle at all.

That thought hangs in my head as we trudge through the dirt. We continue to hang back, just out of earshot of the others, which isn't entirely coincidental. I hope we're almost there.

"This sucks," Lindsay comments as her right boot sinks into a puddle of mud. "This is *not* what I had in mind for this trip."

"Well," I say, "you wanted to get away from civilization, right?"

"No!" She seems affronted by this suggestion. "I just wanted to get Warner away from the hospital for a week. I wanted him all to myself."

I look at the three men up ahead. Warner's blond hair is almost gleaming. He definitely has the best butt of the three of them. And even though we're in the middle of nowhere, he walks forward without any hesitation. I have to admire his confidence.

"So you really like him, huh?" I ask carefully.

A smile lights Lindsay's face. "I really do. I don't think I've ever felt this way about somebody before. He's… perfect."

"Yeah, but…" I step gingerly over a branch on the ground. "What was the deal with lunch? Why wouldn't he let you have a burger?"

She narrows her eyes. "What do you mean?"

"I mean…" I don't want to hurt Lindsay's feelings, but at the same time, I want to make sure she's not with a guy who's going to break her heart. Or manipulate her. I owe her that much. "You wanted to get a burger, and he told you not to. Then you got that teeny tiny salad instead."

"Oh." She waves her hand. "That has nothing to do with him. I'm trying to lose some weight, that's all."

"You don't need to lose any weight!" I don't point out the obvious, which is that she's at least twenty pounds skinnier than I am. If she needs to lose weight, I'm in big trouble.

"Bullshit." Lindsay holds out her bare upper arm and grabs a handful of flesh. "Look at this! Warner does not have an ounce of fat on him. It's…embarrassing."

"And why was he looking at you like that when he mentioned boob jobs?" I press her.

"Well…" Lindsay glances down at her chest. "You have to admit, I'm not exactly well endowed."

I'm so upset I nearly trip over a branch on the ground. "Did he *say* that to you?"

"He didn't have to!" She rubs her neck, pushing away sweaty strands of blond hair. "I mean, it's a fact. And I should be grateful he's nice enough to offer me a free surgery. How many guys would do that?"

I make a face. "None."

"Claire…"

Everything she's saying is making me uneasy. It's not like I married such a great guy, but I have to hand it to Noah, he was never judgmental about my looks. He always used to act like I was the most beautiful woman in the world. He certainly never suggested I should lose weight or have *plastic surgery*. And now…well, obviously he doesn't act like he thinks I'm all that attractive anymore. But he doesn't say anything *negative* about my looks, at least.

Who am I kidding? I can't throw stones.

"As long as you think he's a good guy," I finally say. When we get to the hotel, we'll have to talk more about this. I need to make sure she doesn't proceed with an impulse boob job.

"He is, Claire." She takes a deep breath. "In fact…"

"What?"

She ducks under a low-hanging tree branch, and a leaf comes free in her hair. "I think he's going to propose to me this week!"

"Oh." My heart sinks at this revelation. "That's… wonderful! And you…you want to marry him?"

"Of course!"

"I thought you loved being single." Even though Lindsay was my maid of honor, she was never that into weddings or the idea of getting married. She loved her job and her freedom. She dated sometimes, and a few of her boyfriends seemed head over heels in love with her, but she never seemed the slightest bit interested in settling down. And my own marriage hasn't exactly provided her with a shining example of how wonderful it is to be tied to another person.

"Well, I did," she says thoughtfully. "But that was because all the guys I dated were such losers. Warner is perfect. I'm so glad I waited."

I plaster my best smile on my face, hoping she doesn't notice it's phony. It's obvious that when Warner pops the question, Lindsay is going to say yes. There's nothing I can do about it.

CHAPTER 10

CLAIRE

I have to pee again.

It was bad enough when I was in the car and I knew Noah was going to yell at me. But this is so much worse. Where am I supposed to go to the bathroom around here? I don't foresee us running into a Porta-John anytime in the near future.

"Lindsay," I murmur. "Do you...do you need to go to the bathroom?"

"Yes!" she cries. "Oh my God, *desperately*! What are we supposed to do?"

"I think..." I take a deep breath. "I guess we'll have to go in the woods."

Lindsay bites her lip. "I don't know if I can do that, Claire."

I don't know if I can either. But I'm not seeing much of a choice at this point. There's only so long I can hold it.

"We have to tell the guys to wait for us." I squint at

them, far ahead of us—and getting farther and farther every second. "Jack! Noah!"

"Warner!" Lindsay calls.

Naturally, Noah ignores me. But after a few seconds, Jack turns around and waves at us. "Everything okay?" he calls back.

I don't want to yell over to them that Lindsay and I need the bathroom. So I jog over and Lindsay follows close behind. "We need the bathroom," I say quietly as soon as I'm within earshot.

Noah doesn't comment on how I should've used the bathroom back at the diner. He's just lucky he's a guy. They have it so much easier. They don't even have to pull down their pants.

Warner's gaze darts between the trees. "There are no bathrooms around here."

"I know," I say tightly. "But we need to stop and… you know…"

"Oh." Jack shoves his hands into his pockets. "Well, we'll wait over here for you. Take your time."

I glance off into the woods. I really, really don't want to do this. "But how…?"

Warner smirks. "You squat. It's not hard, ladies."

I cannot believe this is how my day is going. Part of me wants to just say to hell with it, I'll hold it in. But another part of me is worried that a violent sneeze will soak my shorts. And it's not like I have a change of clothes.

"Fine," I say. "Michelle, do you need to go?"

"No, thanks," she says.

Of course she doesn't need to go. The woman is a robot.

I squeeze my hands together. "Okay then."

"Try to stand facing downhill," Jack says. "I've heard it reduces the chances of getting urine on your clothing."

Noah snorts at the look on my face. He thinks it's hilarious I have to do this. Well, to hell with him. I'll squat if I have to.

At least I've got a pack of tissues in my purse.

Lindsay and I go find a private area to do our business. I pick a tree that looks thick enough to conceal me, and Lindsay does the same. I pull my shorts down and go as carefully as I can manage. Considering I've never done this before, I think I do a fair job.

After I zip my shorts up, I grab onto the tree for balance, the wood biting into my palm. As I pull my hand away, I notice five deep grooves in the splintered bark.

Claw marks.

These marks weren't made by a little bunny. The marks are long and deep. The claws that broke the bark were obviously extremely sharp. And there's a second set of claw marks above the first. Was something climbing the tree?

I raise my eyes. I see nothing but leaves above me. But behind me, I hear a rustling sound.

"Claire?"

I nearly jump out of my skin at the sound of Lindsay's voice. She's standing behind me, hugging her chest. "Is everything okay? Were you able to pee?"

I run my fingers over the deep grooves in the bark. "Look at this."

Lindsay's eyes widen as she stares at the distinctive marks. "Oh my God. What animal do you think did it?"

I have no idea. All I know is I don't want to come across the animal that made that.

I have this overpowering urge to keep moving, but Lindsay insists on going back to the others to show them the claw marks. I follow her, but I don't really want to keep looking at those marks. I want to get as far away as possible from the animal that made them.

Jack is rolling his eyes until he sees the marks on the tree. For a moment, he looks rattled. He runs his hand over the deep grooves. "Wow," he says.

"Do you think it's a bear?" Lindsay asks.

"Maybe." Jack frowns at the claw marks as he runs his hand over them. "Black bears are known for marking trees. But..."

I raise my eyebrows. "What?"

"I would think claw marks from a bear would be a lot higher up on the tree," he says. "It could have been a small bear. Or...something else."

I don't know whether to feel better or worse about it. Bears are scary. But at the same time, their behavior is predictable. We know what bears are capable of. We don't know what some mystery animal with long, sharp claws is capable of.

"Anyway..." Jack takes a step back from the tree. "Most animals that mark trees do it to mark their territory. So if this is the territory of some large animal, we should move on."

That sounds like a very good idea to me.

CHAPTER 11

CLAIRE

Three hours later, we are not at the inn. We are not anywhere near the inn. In spite of Warner's map and Jack's compass, we are utterly lost.

And it's going to get dark soon.

Lindsay begs until we stop for a quick rest. Noah's water is long gone, and we all take sips from Jack's water bottle. I feel slightly ill at the knowledge that when this water bottle is empty, we won't have anything to drink. Even though the sun has fallen in the sky, it's still hot out. My shirt is soaked with sweat. I could easily polish off the entire bottle by myself. My mouth feels like the Sahara.

Jack takes this opportunity to reassure us. He looks tired and sweaty but not nearly as frazzled as Lindsay and I look. His shaggy dark hair is slightly damp, and it's sexy. I can't wait to get this guy alone at the inn.

If we ever get there.

"It's going to be fine," Jack says to us. "We made a

wrong turn so we have to backtrack. But we're on target. We'll be there before dark."

"It really feels like we're lost," I say.

"We're *not* lost." Jack's voice is warm and reassuring. He starts to reach for my hand but then catches himself. "Look, we're going to hit civilization at some point soon, like it or not. These days, it's very hard to get lost in the woods. And it's even harder to stay lost."

I reach into my purse and pull out my cell phone. I'm hoping to see a bar of reception or maybe a missed call from Penny. But there's still no service.

"We should have stayed in the car." Lindsay's eyes are red-rimmed. Her hands are shaky as she wrings them together. "We have no idea where we are."

"No," Warner says. "*You* have no idea where you are, Lindsay. Jack and I know exactly where we are."

He sounds like an arrogant jerk when he says it, but God, I hope he's right.

I look up at Noah. He has been privy to all the navigating, and he doesn't look nearly as confident as the other two guys. Our eyes meet for a moment, and he shakes his head almost imperceptibly. There was a time when I could have gone up to him and asked him to tell me what's really going on, but that's not going to happen right now. That headshake is the best I'm going to get. And anyway, it tells me everything I need to know:

We are screwed.

Lindsay jerks up her head. "Did you hear that?"

"Hear what?" Warner asks.

She hugs her chest. "It was like…a growl or a howl or…"

I shiver despite the heat. We haven't come across any wild animals aside from a lot of bugs and a few rabbits. But there were those claw marks on the tree. Obviously, there are wild animals around here. Big ones.

"I didn't hear it," Jack says.

Lindsay's hands ball into fists. "Well, I did!"

Jack seems sure of himself, but I'm not so certain. Don't people lost in the woods get attacked by animals all the time? Is that so far-fetched?

"Look, there are probably bears around here," Jack says. "Mostly black bears. But, you know, bears are usually scared of humans. Unless they feel cornered or their children are threatened, they're not going to attack."

"Great, that's real comforting," Lindsay mutters.

"Can we get going again?" Michelle speaks up. She shifts her purse, which is bulging with the weight of her laptop. She refused to leave it behind. "I have a ton of work to do tonight, and I need to charge this thing."

I look over at Lindsay, whose shoulders are sagging. I can tell she's reluctant to venture deeper into the woods, but we don't have much of a choice—it's not like we can stay behind. I don't know how they're ever going to find us again if we don't stay together. The woods seem endless.

"All right," she finally says. "Let's go."

My feet are starting to ache from all the walking. I didn't realize how out of shape I was until this hike. When was the last time I went hiking? Actually, have I *ever* been hiking? It doesn't seem like the sort of thing Noah and I would have ever done. We were more the Netflix-and-chill type of couple. It used to work for us. We were both a couple of couch potatoes.

Jack told me we were going to hike together during the trip. At the time, it sounded romantic. I liked the idea of being lost in the woods with Jack. But right now, when we are *actually* lost in the woods, it doesn't seem even remotely romantic. I think the hike is officially canceled. Once I get to that hotel, I'm not setting foot in the wilderness. I might not even leave the room.

Lindsay is walking even slower than I am. She does not look good—her complexion is distinctly pale. Her stylishly messy bun from earlier is now just messy, and there are loose hairs plastered to the back of her neck. Before today, I'm not sure I ever saw Lindsay sweat, but now there's a V of sweat along the neck of her shirt. Then again, I'm not sure I look much better.

The two of us are lagging a good twenty feet behind the others. We're far enough back that I can't hear a word they're saying. But I make sure to always keep them in my line of sight. The last thing I want is to get separated.

"When we get to the inn," Lindsay says, "I'm going to soak in the bathtub for, like, five hours. Until I'm a *prune*."

I manage a smile. "I just want to lie down on a nice soft bed."

"You know what else I'm going to do?" Lindsay licks her lips. "I'm going to order room service. A nice big bacon cheeseburger."

I laugh. "Goodness, what will Warner say?"

"And a big box of double-stuffed Oreo cookies for dessert." She inhales sharply. "God, I haven't eaten Oreos in…years, I think."

Back in college, I would have said that Oreo cookies were Lindsay's favorite food in the whole world. She always had a box of them in her room, in various stages of being eaten. She used to take them apart and make a little stack of the chocolate wafers, then a giant ball of the creamy stuffing. I remember the way I used to groan when Lindsay would pop that white ball in her mouth.

Okay, I used to do it too sometimes. But it was *fun*. I can't imagine Warner would approve of Lindsay eating a giant ball of Oreo stuffing.

"Honestly…" Lindsay rubs at a little red patch on her neck. Now that the sun is falling, the bugs are coming out, which stinks for me—I'm always a target. "I am *so* hungry right now. I feel like I could eat bugs."

"Jack has some beef jerky in his bag, you know."

Her eyes light up for a moment, but then she shakes her head. "Warner will kill me."

"Warner will kill you if you eat some beef jerky when you're lost in the woods?"

"You don't get it." She smacks at her neck, then looks at her palm. "God damn it. There's, like, a million mosquitoes out here."

"What don't I get?"

"Look, I just…" Lindsay seems like she has something to say, but before she gets it out, she points excitedly at a bush on the ground. "Claire! It's blueberries!"

I look at where she's pointing. It's a large, leafy green bush that has a bunch of plump, dark-blue berries growing from it. Even though I had a burger rather than a salad, the sight of any sort of food makes my stomach growl. It's past our usual dinnertime.

"Are you sure those are blueberries?" I ask.

"Of course! I used to go blueberry picking all the time when I was a kid." She plucks a berry off the bush. "This is definitely a blueberry."

"I don't know…" I look ahead at the others, who are

within earshot, but only if we shout. "Maybe we should ask Jack if they're okay to eat."

"Why? Because he was a Boy Scout a million years ago?" She throws up her arms. "He has no clue. If he did, we'd have found that stupid inn by now."

Before I can stop her, she pops the picked berry into her mouth. She chews on it thoughtfully. I take a step forward, ready to catch her if she starts foaming at the mouth and collapses.

"It tastes good!" she says. "It's a blueberry, Claire. It's ripe and sweet. If it were poison, it would taste *bad*."

Is that true? I feel certain I read some poison berries have a sweet taste.

Lindsay is plucking berries from the bush. She's got at least a dozen of them in her hand, and she's eating them as she goes. I get a sick feeling in my stomach. This is a bad idea. As much as I'm not excited by the idea of Jack's beef jerky, I don't think we should be eating random berries we find in the woods. Also, don't blueberries ripen in July? It's still only June.

"Lindsay," I murmur, "I really don't think this is a good idea. We have no idea if the berries are safe or not. Can't we just check with Jack?"

"Oh, come on. What are the chances some random berries we come across are poison?"

Maybe I'm a glass-half-empty type of person, but I feel like there's a much smaller chance that some random berries in the woods *aren't* poison. "Lindsay…"

"Fine." She pops a couple more berries in her mouth, then drops the rest in the dirt below us. "I won't eat them, okay? Happy?"

I look up—everyone else is way ahead of us. They

don't seem at all concerned we've fallen so far behind. Would they even notice if we just vanished? "We better catch up."

"Yeah." Lindsay looks suddenly exhausted, like she can't go another step. "We better."

I know exactly how she feels. But we don't have much of a choice. If we want to get out of here tonight, we've got to keep walking.

CHAPTER 12

ANONYMOUS

My mother grew berries in our backyard.

She grew mostly blueberries and raspberries. The raspberries started as tiny, hard, green blobs, then would expand and darken in color. Those were my favorites. When they were ripe, you could pluck them right off the bush with no effort at all.

The blueberries would ripen a month after the raspberries. They would start out pale, then get fat and turn blue. The blueberries tasted good, but I avoided them. Because of the nightshade.

My mother grew deadly nightshade in our backyard.

The name of the plant is *Atropa belladonna*. It's part of the nightshade family, generally found in Europe, North Africa, and Western Asia. But you can find it in some parts of America too.

Belladonna berries look very much like blueberries. They're shiny black, about half an inch in size, and they're sweet.

The berries are highly toxic. They cause delirium and hallucinations, and they disrupt the body's ability to regulate its sweating, heart rate, and breathing. Eventually, seizures and cardiovascular failure will occur. Early humans made poisonous arrows using belladonna. In an adult, fifteen to twenty berries are enough to kill you. A child could die from two or three.

My mother grew the deadly nightshade because she wanted to discourage anyone from sneaking into our backyard and stealing berries. She secretly hoped to find a child lying dead in the backyard, a handful of berries clutched in their hand.

When I was in the backyard, I could tell the difference. I knew what the plant looked like. But in a bowl, belladonna and blueberries look almost identical.

When I was about seven years old, my dad returned from a business trip to Chicago in the early hours of Sunday morning. My mom always spent forever getting dressed up when he was returning from a trip. She was in a pink sundress, and her white-blond hair was all loose and curled instead of limp and oily. When she made an effort, my mother could be very beautiful.

We spent ages cleaning the house top to bottom. My fingers ached from scrubbing, and my eyes still burned from the cleaning fluid fumes. She even spent twenty minutes brushing our cat, Snowball, until her white fur was gleaming. Snowball looked better than I did, but that was often the case.

The three of us were waiting at the front door when my dad walked in with his luggage, slight circles under his brown eyes. "What a greeting!" he exclaimed. He had a big, loud voice and a bigger smile. It made everyone like him. He was a good salesman.

My mother smiled at him with her bright-red lips. "And I made you a big breakfast of bacon and eggs."

"I can't wait!"

But instead of following my mom into the kitchen like she wanted, he started rifling around in his bag. She frowned and put her hands on her hips. "Come on, John. The food will be cold."

"Hang on." He dug around for another few seconds, then pulled out a Bulls baseball cap. The angry red bull stared at me from the jet-black cap. "Here you go, sport."

My dad traveled a lot, and for every city he went to, he brought me back a baseball cap. I had a big collection now. I took the cap and stuck it on my head. "Wow! Thanks!"

"And I got some other stuff for you," he said.

"John." My mother's voice was tight. "Why don't we do this after we eat?"

"It'll just be a minute, Helen."

It was great when he brought me back stuff from his trip. It didn't make up for not seeing him for days or even a week at a time, but it was something to look forward to. My mom didn't like it though. She stormed off while he gave me my presents.

It was a few minutes later when we got to the kitchen table. My father's eggs and bacon were laid out on a white ceramic plate with a heaping glass of orange juice. And there was also a bowl of cereal on the table that hadn't been there before.

My mother beamed at us. "I made breakfast for both of you."

I sat down in front of the bowl of cereal. It was corn-flakes, like I had for breakfast most days, but usually I made it myself. My mom never offered to make me breakfast before, but today she had done it without being asked. I looked down at the bowl—she had poured in too much milk, and the cornflakes would be soggy. She had also sprinkled in a handful of berries.

"I put in some blueberries from the garden," she said.

I pulled the Bulls cap low on my forehead as I stared down at the bowl of cereal. The berries were dark blue. They looked like blueberries.

I pushed the berries around the bowl with my spoon. My mom watched me. "What's wrong? Why aren't you eating?"

My dad was already digging into his plate of food. "Eat up, sport. It's good for you."

I pushed my spoon around a little more until one of the berries rolled right out of my bowl. It teetered on the edge of the table, then finally dropped to the floor. Within a second, Snowball was nosing at the berry. She sniffed at it, and her little pink tongue was poised to take a lick.

"No!" my mother snapped at the cat. Quick as a flash, she scooped the berry up before Snowball could attempt to eat it. "Bad cat. That's not for cats."

My mother loved Snowball. She stroked the cat's white fur gently. She would never let anything happen to Snowball.

Snowball was not allowed to eat the berries.

I took a bite of cornflakes, carefully avoiding the berries. Some of the juice leaked into the milk, but just a tiny amount. I took another bite of cornflakes.

I ate most of the cornflakes, leaving the berries behind. As I pushed my plate away, my mom frowned. "Why didn't you eat the blueberries?"

"I'm not hungry," I mumbled.

"Fruit is good for you," she said. "You have to eat it."

My dad nodded. He had no idea. "Your mother is right. Eat the blueberries."

I looked up at my mom. She had a smile on her lips just for me. When she looked at me that way, I got scared. She told me once that she never wanted to have me. My dad's condom broke. I was a mistake. People correct mistakes.

I pressed my lips closed, afraid if I opened them, somebody would stuff deadly nightshade inside.

"Listen," my father said, "if you don't do what your mother says and finish your breakfast, I'm taking the baseball hat back."

I wanted to tell him the truth—the berries were poison. But he wouldn't believe it. And I would be in even worse trouble.

So I took off the Bulls hat and threw it on the table. Then I ran up to my room.

I got in trouble that day. But I didn't die.

Thanks to my mom, I know everything there is to know about poison berries.

CHAPTER 13

CLAIRE

The sun has fallen in the sky, and we still haven't reached the inn. My feet throb within my sneakers—I'm certain I have a blister on my right big toe. It's a supreme effort just to get my feet to move forward. *Right, left, right, left.* And it doesn't feel like we're making any progress whatsoever. Where the hell is this place?

I take out my phone for what feels like the hundredth time and check to see if there's any reception. There isn't. I'm getting so sick of that "No service" message.

I wonder what the kids are doing. I hope they're okay. I mean, I'm sure Penny is taking good care of them, but they're almost certainly expecting a call from me by now. I hope Emma isn't freaking out too badly.

I had a dream you got eaten by a monster.

"Are you okay, Claire?"

I look over at Jack, who has fallen into step beside me. Lindsay went to catch up with Warner about twenty minutes ago, and he's giving her a ride on his back. Her hiking boots are pretty but not particularly comfortable. I wish I could get a ride on somebody's back. Jack can't offer when Michelle is around. And there's no chance Noah would offer. I'm lucky he doesn't push me off a cliff.

"I've been better," I admit. I take a deep breath. "Are we almost there, you think?"

Jack nods and shows me his compass. "According to the map, if we keep walking due west, it's about half a mile."

Thank God. I can't take much more of this. I'll walk this last half a mile, then I'm going to collapse at the entrance to the hotel.

Of course, what if he's wrong? We've been walking for hours, and every time we ask, the boys say we're "almost there." I shiver.

"Are you cold?" he asks me.

I start to say no, but then I realize I *am* pretty cold. It was so hot when the sun was in the sky, but now that it's down, it's become downright nippy. I look down and see goose bumps all over my arms. And naturally, I don't have any sort of sweatshirt or coat. It didn't seem necessary when the temperature was pushing ninety.

"I'm okay," I say.

He pokes me in the arm. "You've got goose bumps."

I look up, making sure Noah and Michelle are a safe distance ahead of us. I don't want Noah to see Jack touching me or teasing me. "Maybe a little."

"Here." Jack pulls his backpack off and rifles through it. He yanks out a gray hoodie sweatshirt. "Put this on."

I hesitate. "I'm not that cold."

"Come on. Don't be a hero."

I nearly refuse the second time, but then a breeze

washes over us. It *is* pretty cold out. And it's only going to get worse as the night goes on. I should just take the sweatshirt. What's the difference? Just because Jack gave me a sweatshirt, that doesn't mean we're sleeping together. It's just a nice gesture between friends.

So I take the sweatshirt and pull it over my head. It's soft and warm and it smells like wood chips. I smile up at him. "Thanks."

"Anything for my Claire."

Of course, I'm not *his* Claire. Currently, I'm Noah's Claire, but that won't be true after this week. Getting lost in the woods has only strengthened my resolution to end things with Noah. Life is too short to stay together for the kids.

Unfortunately, Jack will never leave Michelle. Not because he loves her so much but because she's a divorce lawyer. How do you leave your divorce lawyer wife? You can't. But I don't care. Either way, I want to be free from my own marriage.

I squint up ahead and see that Warner has lowered Lindsay to the ground. She's sitting down on a fallen tree, doubled over. Noah and Michelle are talking to her, and she keeps shaking her head. I jog over to see what's going on.

"Lindsay," I say, "what's going on? Are you okay?"

She looks up at me. Her blue eyes are bloodshot and her usually porcelain complexion is now slightly green. "My stomach is upset. I think it's all the bouncing."

"You don't look very good," Warner says.

"I'm fine," Lindsay insists. "I just need fifteen minutes to sit."

I look down at Lindsay's stylish hiking boots. Her

right foot is planted next to an ant hill, and several large carpenter ants are crawling up her leg. She doesn't even seem to notice, even when one of those ants hops onto her forearm. She must really be sick.

Michelle looks down at her watch. "Christ, the whole night is killed. We're never going to get there at any reasonable hour."

Noah starts to roll his eyes at me, but then, when he looks at me, he does a double take. His hazel eyes widen, and it takes a second to realize he's looking at my sweatshirt. Or should I say, *Jack's* sweatshirt.

But he couldn't possibly recognize Jack's sweatshirt. It's just a nondescript gray hoodie.

"You guys don't need to fuss over me," Lindsay says. "I'll be fine. I just need to rest."

"Rest?" Warner repeats. "Lindsay, I was *carrying* you."

I'm waiting to see what Lindsay is going to say back to her boyfriend, but then I feel Noah's fingers close around my forearm, and he tugs me a few paces back. His lips lean in close to my ear. "Hey," he says. "Where did you get that sweatshirt?"

Damn it.

"Um," I say.

"Is that *Jack's* sweatshirt?" he asks.

I could lie, but that might make it worse. If I've got nothing to hide, why would I lie? "Yeah. I was cold and he had an extra sweatshirt, so…"

Noah blinks a few times and tugs at the sweatshirt he's wearing. "If you were cold, I would have…"

"Would you?"

He opens his mouth, but before he can get any words out, we hear a bloodcurdling scream.

91

CHAPTER 14

CLAIRE

The scream came from Lindsay. She's gotten to her feet, and she's pointing into the distance.

"Lindsay!" Warner is doing his best to calm her down. "Stop screaming. What's wrong?"

"It was a bear!" Her blue eyes are flashing. "I saw it! It was coming toward us! It had huge claws and giant white fangs!"

We all turn to look in the direction she's pointing with her shaking hand. It's gotten pretty dark now, but it doesn't look like there's anything there. Only blackness, branches, and leaves. Now that she's stopped screaming, all we can hear are crickets chirping. An owl hoots in the distance.

Once again, I flash back to Emma's words. *I dreamed you got eaten up by a monster.*

I think of those claw marks on the tree. Despite Jack's sweatshirt, I shiver and hug my chest.

"A bear isn't going to just attack us out of nowhere," Jack says patiently.

"How do you know that?" There's something wild and unfamiliar in Lindsay's eyes. "That bear is going to kill us all! I know it!"

"Jesus," Jack mutters under his breath.

Lindsay clutches her belly and drops back down onto the fallen tree. She lets out a low moan. She's acting so strangely. I can't imagine what's gotten into her, except...

"Lindsay ate some wild berries," I blurt out.

Jack's head snaps up. "Wild berries?"

"Blueberries," I say. "About an hour ago. Maybe a little more."

"Lindsay!" Warner cries. "Is that true?"

She lifts her head and nods miserably. "It wasn't a big deal."

"How could you do something so stupid?" Warner's handsome face turns pink. "Eating wild berries in the middle of a forest? Why would you do something like that?"

"I was so hungry," she whimpers. "I just had a few."

He shakes his head. "And now look what's happened to you."

Jack's forehead is crumpled in concern. "Claire, what did the berries look like?"

"They were blue," I say helplessly. I try to remember those tiny berries that Lindsay was stuffing in her mouth. "*Bluish*, at least."

"How many did she eat?"

I lift my shoulders. "I'm not entirely sure. Ten? Maybe fifteen?"

"Shit," Jack breathes.

"What?" My heart flutters in my chest. "What do you think it was?"

Jack just shakes his head and crouches down next to Lindsay, who looks even worse than she did a minute ago. She's doubled over, and I feel a stab of guilt in my chest. Lindsay was begging me to stay in the car with her. If only I had done it…

"Hey." Noah touches my arm to get my attention. "*You* didn't eat any berries, did you?"

Is that concern in his eyes? "No. I didn't."

Thank God.

Lindsay is deteriorating rapidly. She's becoming lethargic, and Warner is rubbing her shoulder, trying to get her to answer questions. I comfort myself with the fact that he's a doctor. We've got a licensed physician with us—a *surgeon*. Even if Lindsay ate some poison berries, he'll be able to save her.

"She's losing consciousness." Warner's voice is even, but there's a note of underlying panic. "We need to lie her down."

Lindsay's eyes are closed, and she mumbles something incoherent. Jack and Warner lower her down onto the dirt, and she's like a rag doll. Her face looks really pale.

"What the hell did she eat?" Warner mutters.

"Could be elderberry," Jack says. "But I'm more worried it could've been deadly nightshade. I've heard of that growing out here."

I squeeze my hands together. "Nightshade?"

"The berries are sort of purple-black," Jack says. "They look like blueberries a little bit. And if she ate that…"

He doesn't complete his sentence. He doesn't have to.

Lindsay's body suddenly goes rigid on the ground. Jack takes several steps back, clearly shaken, but Warner stays close to her. I am frozen, watching in horror as Lindsay's body starts to shake violently.

"She's having a seizure," Warner says. "This isn't good."

Well duh.

The shaking goes on for what seems like forever, and when it ends, her body is completely limp. Her head falls to the right, and a glob of drool oozes from the corner of her lips. Warner places his hand on her chest, then lowers his head to the level of her mouth.

"Shit," he says. "She's not breathing."

I clasp my hand over my mouth. "She's not…"

I take a step back, watching helplessly as Warner performs CPR on Lindsay. I watch his muscular arms pumping against her frail chest. He counts quietly to fifteen with each compression, then exhales two breaths into her mouth. Every minute or so, he stops and looks at her chest, then takes her pulse.

Thank God Warner is here. He knows what he's doing. He's going to save her.

Noah is standing beside me, watching with the same horrified expression that I must have on my own face. At some point, I feel his arm go around my shoulders. I barely notice it.

"She'll be okay," he murmurs.

"Does anybody have cell signal?" Warner calls out between compressions.

My hands are trembling as I pull my phone out of my pocket. I say a quiet prayer to myself. But it's just as I thought. No service.

Noah has his phone in his hand. My eyes light up when I notice he has a single bar. But then he shakes his head. "No service," he says.

I must be hallucinating. I'm seeing mirages of bars on cell phones.

Warner works on her for another ten minutes. I am frozen in place, watching him. He repeats the same process over and over. Compressions, breath, compressions, breath, check for breathing, check for a pulse. Each time he checks, I hold my breath, hoping he'll say she's back. *She's okay.*

But then he collapses onto the dirt beside her. He put his hands on his knees and stares down at her, his eyes glassy. "I think…she's gone."

"Gone?" I cry. "What are you talking about?"

Warner lifts his watery eyes to look at me. "She's dead."

"No!" I squirm away from Noah and drop down beside Lindsay. I pick up her limp left hand. "That's not possible! All she did was eat a few berries."

"If it was nightshade—" Jack says.

"Shut up!" I scream. "The only reason she ate those berries is because we've been lost in the damn woods for hours! Why can't we find this stupid inn? Why can't we…"

I can't even finish my sentence because I'm crying so hard. How could this be happening? We're supposed to be lying in the Jacuzzi now with a glass of bubbly. Instead, we're lost in the woods and Lindsay is dead. *Dead!* How could Lindsay be dead? She's my best friend! My college roommate. My maid of honor. The children's godmother. She was so young and healthy and…

I feel Jack's arms around me. I sob into his chest like I haven't cried in years. Why did I go on this trip? I don't know anything about the wilderness. I just wanted a week away. Is that really so awful?

Oh, Lindsay.

When I pull away from Jack, there are wet spots on his shirt from my leaking eyes, rimmed with mascara. For a moment, I try to get control of my emotions, but there's no hope of that. My legs give out beneath me, and I fall to the ground. I squeeze handfuls of dirt in my palms as I gasp for air.

"Lindsay," I whisper.

She looks so still, lying there. It seems impossible to believe she's gone.

I met Lindsay on my first day of college. I had been so nervous about my new roommate—I got butterflies whenever I thought about it. I had heard so many horror stories from people about bad roommates, and then, when Lindsay walked in with her cute blond bob and shy smile, I couldn't help but throw my arms around her. She laughed and hugged me back.

Lindsay will never hug me back again.

When the kids were born, there was nobody else I would've considered asking to be their godmother. The kids adore their aunt Lindsay. Even though we've grown apart a bit since I embraced suburban life, she's always got an armful of presents for them when she comes over.

What will I tell Aidan and Emma?

"Claire?" It's Jack's voice. "Are you okay?"

"No!" I bury my face in my hands. "I'm not okay!"

This is all my fault. Lindsay wanted to stay behind, and I said no. I said we should stay with the group. If only I had stayed behind in the car with Lindsay, she'd be alive right now. Or if I had tried harder to talk her out of eating those berries…

I want to give up. I feel like lying down in the dirt and not going another step.

"What are we going to do next?" Michelle pipes up.

That's Michelle all over. My best friend is lying on the

ground *dead*, her body not even cold yet, and Michelle is plotting our next move. I lift my head to glare at her. Of the five of us, she seems the least frazzled by far. Her black hair doesn't have a strand out of place, and even her makeup is intact.

I shoot daggers at her with my eyes. "What's the difference?"

"What's the difference?" she repeats. She gives me a sharp look that reminds me that I probably shouldn't have been clinging to her husband for comfort. I hadn't been thinking about it at the time, but now I realize how that must've looked to everyone else—especially Michelle. The truth is I'm scared of this woman. "The difference is that *we're still lost*. We don't have much food or water, and it's now nighttime. We need to keep moving."

I scramble back to my feet. "We can't leave Lindsay here."

Michelle stares at me. "She's *dead*, Claire. And if we don't get moving, we will be too."

I shake my head.

"I'm surprised at you." Michelle clucks her tongue. "You've got two young children waiting for you at home. You really don't care about getting back safely for them?"

I suck in a breath. She makes a good point. If I had eaten those berries like Lindsay, I could be lying on the ground beside her—dead. Emma and Aidan wouldn't have a mother anymore. All of a sudden, my longing for my children becomes so intense that I feel like I'm suffocating.

But at the same time, I can't imagine leaving Lindsay here like this. Just lying on the ground. What if animals start *eating* her? I feel sick at the thought of scavengers chewing at her skin. She doesn't deserve that. Even if she's dead.

Oh God, I can't believe she's dead. Lindsay, Lindsay…

"Warner," I say pleadingly. He looked so haunted when he pulled away from Lindsay's dead body. There's no way he's going to want to keep moving. "You think we should stay, don't you?"

Warner wipes his eyes with the back of his hand. He looks down at Lindsay, his light-brown eyebrows scrunched together.

"I…" He clears his throat. "I actually…I think Michelle is right. We have to keep moving."

I stare at him in disbelief. "What? Are you serious?"

He lets out a long sigh. "We have to. It's our only hope. That's what Lindsay would've wanted."

My mouth falls open. I can't believe other people are agreeing to this. Especially Warner, the guy who was sleeping with Lindsay and apparently so in love with her that he was going to pop the question this week. He should be showing a little more grief for the woman he almost married. He should be sobbing into his hands. Not spouting bullshit about how Lindsay would've wanted us to abandon her body here in the middle of the woods.

"You're kidding," I say. "Aren't you *sad*? Can't we take five damn minutes to grieve?"

His full lips purse. "What do you want me to say? I'm sad. Of course I'm sad. Lindsay was a beautiful woman. This was tragic." He takes a deep breath. "But it's not going to help Lindsay for us to die here."

I look over at Jack. He hasn't said a word about any of this. But he'll support me. He's known Lindsay almost as long as I have. And he cares about me more than anyone else in this group, including my own husband. Not for the first time, I wonder what sort of life I would have had if I had ditched Noah for Jack at that party in college. "Jack?"

"I agree with Michelle and Warner," he says quietly. "We need to keep moving."

I jerk my head back like I've been slapped. I know they're just being logical, of course. It's not like I *want* to be stuck out here in the wilderness. It's not like I want to starve to death or die of thirst. I want to go home to my family. But at the same time, I just can't fathom leaving Lindsay like this.

But what am I supposed to do? Stay here alone with a dead body?

"As soon as we get to the inn," Jack says, "we'll send somebody to…collect her."

"*Collect* her?" How could he be so cold? "What if they can't find her? Or what if it's too late and she's already been…"

I can't even bring myself to say the words. I can't think about scavengers ripping apart my best friend's dead body. I try to look into Jack's brown eyes, but he averts his gaze.

"Let's get moving," Warner says. "It shouldn't be much longer."

Jack shifts his backpack on his shoulders and follows Warner. Michelle does the same. I stand there, looking down at Lindsay's motionless body. I can't just leave her. I *can't*.

"Hey."

I turn my head and see Noah standing behind me. Somehow, I'd almost forgotten he was with us. He backed away when I was clinging to Jack. If he says a word about that, I swear to God, I will lose it completely.

"Hey," I manage around the lump in my throat.

"Listen." He rubs at the back of his neck. "If you want to stay behind, I'll stay with you."

I blink at him—it's the last thing I expected him to say. "You will?"

He nods. "Yeah, you…you shouldn't be alone here."

I look ahead. The others have gained a lot of distance on us already. If we wait much longer, we won't be able to catch up anymore. Whatever I decide, I have to decide right now.

"Do you think I'm being stupid for wanting to stay behind?" I ask.

Noah shakes his head. "Lindsay was your best friend. I don't blame you." He sighs. "It all doesn't feel real, you know?"

I nod. I look ahead again to the others. I feel awful about what happened to Lindsay. But it could've easily been me lying on the ground right now. I dodged a bullet.

For now, at least. The scary reality is we don't have much water, and we can't survive long without it. I imagine Penny telling my children that their parents didn't make it home. That they'll have to grow up without us. I imagine the way their faces would crumble.

I have to keep moving. For Emma and Aidan.

"I think we should stay with the others," I finally say.

"Okay," he agrees.

I pick a wildflower from the ground. It's Lindsay's favorite color—purple. I gently lay the flower down on her chest. I kiss my fingertips, then gently press them against Lindsay's cheek. She still feels warm, but in another hour or two, her body will be cold. I don't want to think about it. I straighten up and start walking in the direction the others went. Noah follows beside me, although keeping a respectful distance.

"Thanks for offering to stay," I say to him.

He's quiet for a moment. "I'm really glad you didn't eat any of those berries."

Me too.

CHAPTER 15

CLAIRE

We've been walking about another hour when I hear a woman's scream from up ahead.

After what happened to Lindsay, my pulse immediately shoots up. I've been walking alone for the last half hour or so. Noah was staying beside me initially, but then he went ahead to see how the navigation process was going. I can't even begin to read the map and the arguments about which way to go were stressing me out, so I stayed behind. I don't feel like talking to anybody anyway—all I can think about is Lindsay. Every time I shut my eyes for a moment, I see her pale face.

My eyes have been mostly downcast, because I'm trying to keep from tripping on any branches. But now I look up sharply, trying to figure out what just happened. The only other person in our group who could have screamed like that is Michelle.

Did she see a wild animal?

I jog to catch up with the others. As I get closer, I see

that Michelle is sitting on the ground, clutching her left ankle. Her face is pink and her jet-black bun has become a little bit unraveled. Even her lipstick has rubbed off. That's a first.

"Are you okay, Michelle?" I ask.

"Do I *look* okay?" she snaps at me.

"Michelle tripped and twisted her ankle," Jack explains.

Suddenly I don't feel so stupid for keeping my eyes on the ground.

Michelle moans and pulls up her pants leg. The ankle already looks swollen—soon it will probably turn purple. I wince at the sight of it. "I can't believe I did that," she groans.

"Can you put weight on it?" Warner asks.

"I'll try." She holds out a hand to Jack, who hauls her to her feet. She gingerly attempts to stand on her left leg and screams again. "Oh my God…"

"It might be broken," Warner says.

"No." Michelle grits her teeth. "I *can't* have a broken ankle." Her eyes fill with tears. "You don't get it. I do *not* have time for this. I don't have time for *any* of this." She lowers herself down to the ground. "I should never have come on this stupid trip. I only came because…"

She lifts her black eyes and stares at me. It's impossible to miss the accusation in that stare. Does she know about me and Jack? Did she only come on the trip so she could keep an eye on us?

I drop my eyes. I can't deal with this right now. I need to focus all my energy on making it to that inn. On surviving so I can get back to my children.

"Does anyone have signal?" Jack asks.

I take out my phone from my purse. I've been checking

periodically, but I haven't looked in at least half an hour. I hold it up—still no service. Worse, the battery is dying. I should probably turn the phone off so I don't drain the battery completely while it's searching for a connection, but I can't make myself do it.

"What am I going to do?" Michelle moans. "I can't walk like this."

"But we've got to find the inn," Warner says. He looks down at his watch. "Once we find it, we'll come back for you."

The panic on Michelle's face is unmistakable. She reaches out and grasps Jack's arm hard enough that he winces. "You can't leave me."

He squirms. "Michelle…"

Her fingers bite into his forearm. I wouldn't be surprised if she drew some blood. "Don't even think about it."

"Okay, okay." He forces a smile. "Look, we're all really tired. I think we should camp here for the night and then start up again when we're fresh in the morning."

"Camp here?" Warner looks at the woods around us, densely populated with trees and branches. Now that it's dark, it's hard to see more than about six feet ahead of us. "You're joking."

As much as I dislike Warner, he has a point. This doesn't seem like a good place to be setting up camp for the night.

Jack looks up. "There was a clearing we passed a few minutes ago. We can camp there. It's just for the night. I can build a fire."

Warner's handsome face darkens. In the moonlight, his perfectly chiseled features look almost frightening. How could poor Lindsay have fallen in love with this man? "We're almost out of food and water, you know. We need to keep moving."

At the mention of food and water, my stomach growls. If I found a bunch of berries right now, I don't think I would be able to resist eating them. But the more pressing need is thirst. Jack has been sharing what was left in his water bottle, but it's not much anymore. I could guzzle the whole thing in one go, but we've got to share it between the five of us.

And then in the morning, we'll have nothing.

"I saw a couple of rabbits traveling north," Jack says. "I'm sure if we follow their footprints, we'll find a water source."

Warner grits his teeth. "Contaminated with God knows what."

As much as Michelle isn't my favorite person, I can't imagine leaving her here. It was hard enough leaving Lindsay. Michelle must be terrified right now. She's holding on to her left ankle with one hand and hugging herself with the other.

It's just dumb luck that Michelle is the one who twisted her ankle instead of me. Even though I've been keeping my eyes on the ground, I've had a few close calls with some stray branches. I could have easily fallen and sprained my ankle. And then I would be the one begging everyone not to abandon me.

"I think we should stay here for the night," I speak up.

"Me too," Noah says.

Warner's face twists into a grimace. He folds his muscular arms across his chest. "You know," he says, "I'm the one with the map."

What is he saying? Is he threatening to go off on his

own with the map, leaving us behind? Frankly, I'd prefer it if he left us alone. He gives me the creeps. I don't know how he fooled Lindsay into thinking he was a good guy— or maybe this situation has brought out his dark side.

Then again, it makes me uneasy to think about being stranded here with no map.

"Look, we're all tired," Jack says. "We'll navigate a lot better when it's light out. And I'm not leaving my wife alone here."

Warner stands there, the wind tousling his golden hair. He looks like he's thinking over what to do next. Finally, he nods. "Fine. We'll sleep here tonight."

It looks like we'll be setting up camp.

CHAPTER 16

CLAIRE

We find the clearing and settle down there. It's not great, but at least it's a solid open space with no trees or prickly branches. Jack suggests gathering leaves to form into makeshift beds for each of us, but it's a far cry from the king-size bed at the inn. If I close my eyes, I can imagine sinking into the silky sheets and memory-foam mattress and pulling the down comforter over me. The image is almost painful.

But the worst part is the realization that I won't get to speak to Emma and Aidan tonight. By now, Penny has probably put them to bed and given up on trying to reach me. I had promised Emma we would talk tonight. I imagine her lying awake in bed, her tiny forehead scrunched up with worry.

I wish I could talk to her. I would give anything to hear her voice for one minute and tell her I'm okay.

I reach into my purse, my hands shaking with desperation. Of course, there's still no service, and the battery is at 5 percent. The next time I take my phone out, the battery might be dead—this could be my last shot. I hold it up in the air, trying desperately to at least get one tiny bar. Just one bar.

Nothing.

I try not to think of my children or my dead best friend as I start gathering as many leaves as I can. As I'm putting together my makeshift bed, I look over at Michelle, whose left ankle is wrapped in an ACE bandage from Jack's first aid kit. Obviously, she can't gather her own leaves.

"Do you want me to make a bed for you?" I offer. I'm trying to make nice, although I'm not sure if the gesture is quite enough to make up for, you know, sleeping with her husband.

Michelle barely lifts her eyes. "Sure."

She could not possibly look less grateful. But then again, Michelle has never been a terribly effusive person. I start gathering some leaves for her anyway. I don't expect her to be falling over herself to thank me. She's injured and probably in pain.

"I sprained my ankle once," I say.

Michelle gives a disinterested grunt.

I pick up a leaf from the ground that's muddier than I thought it was. There's mud smeared all over my hands. It's caked in my fingernails, and there's no way to get it off without a water source. "I was going down some steps in high school," I recall, "and I twisted my ankle on the last step."

She grunts again.

"It happened right before junior prom." I wipe my palms on my shorts. "I remember how upset I was. At the time, it seemed like the worst possible thing that could have happened to me. Isn't that silly?"

109

I look over at Michelle, who is rifling around in her purse.

"Michelle?" I say.

"Oh." She flashes me a bored look. "Sorry, I didn't realize your little story was still going on. What were you asking me?"

"Never mind," I mumble.

Jack returns to our clearing with an arm full of twigs. Michelle rewards him with a big smile, but I wonder if she's just doing it to get on my nerves. Even before Michelle had a reason, she has always disliked me. I felt it from the moment we first met—it was like she took one look at me and decided I wasn't worth her time or energy. But I've never felt that animosity as strongly as I do right now.

I continue gathering leaves as Jack sets about building a fire. Noah helps him gather twigs of various sizes, including a few big ones. Jack makes a little circle of rocks and then carefully places the branches inside in some sort of pattern he learned back in Boy Scouts. I had thought he was going to have to rub two sticks together to make a fire, but thankfully, he brought a lighter. Before too long, we've got a decent fire going.

As I smooth out the leaves on the ground to form Michelle's bed, I hear a sound from off in the distance. I pause, listening. Then I hear it again.

It sounds like a howl.

"What was that?" I ask.

"I didn't hear anything," Jack says.

Goose bumps pop up on my arms despite the fire. It's gotten so cold the last hour. "It sounded like a wolf."

There was a period when Aidan was really into wolves,

when he was writing a paper on them in third grade. He used to randomly spout out facts about wolves. That's how I know that wolves usually travel in packs. So if there's a wolf out there, there's probably more than one.

Jack shakes his head as he pokes at the fire with a stick. "There are no wolves around here."

"How do you know that?"

He shrugs. "There just aren't wolves in these parts."

"Well, maybe they came from *another* part." I look over at Michelle, who is sitting against a tree, her bandaged left leg propped up on her monstrous purse to reduce the swelling. "Did you hear it?"

She doesn't even lift her eyes. "No."

No surprise there.

"Maybe it was the wind," Jack suggests.

It wasn't the wind. It was a wild animal. I know it. I can't help but think of those claw marks on the tree.

Warner comes into the clearing with a few more branches, which he dumps into the fire. I want to ask him if he heard the sound, but I have a feeling the answer is no. I don't need another person to make me feel stupid.

"It could have been a coyote," Jack says. "There are a lot of coyotes around here."

"What could have been a coyote?" Warner asks.

Michelle taps a foot against the ground. "Claire heard a sound. It was probably the wind."

I rub my arms for warmth and try to ignore Michelle. "Are coyotes dangerous?"

"Not usually." Jack shrugs. "They're usually afraid of people. Especially ones in the woods. I doubt they would approach us."

"Unless they're rabid," Warner says.

111

Jack shoots him a look. "There aren't any rabid coyotes in these woods."

"Why not?" Warner cracks his knuckles loudly. "Because you don't want there to be?"

Jack shakes his head. "There just aren't. Anyway, it was probably the wind."

Except I can't get Warner's words out of my head. If a rabid coyote bursts into this clearing, we are done for. We don't have a weapon. That coyote would certainly be able to bite at least one of us before we could overpower it. At least I'm not the sitting duck. If I were Michelle, I'd be terrified right now—the coyote would definitely get her first.

Eventually, we all settle down around the fire. The yellow flames are crackling atop the wood Jack gathered, and the warmth radiates around us. Jack has his arm around Michelle, and she's cuddling up against him. Noah is next to me, but there's no cuddling. I can't remember the last time the two of us cuddled. Hell, we barely touch each other anymore.

Warner is sitting across from me. He's got his legs folded in front of him, and he's staring at the fire with glassy eyes. I wonder if he's thinking about Lindsay. Now that she's not here, he seems really out of place. We barely know the guy, and what I know, I don't like. I wish he could just disappear.

I feel intense itchiness on the left side of my neck, and I smack my hand against it. "I'm getting eaten alive here."

"Yeah." Jack swats at something in the air. "The mosquitoes are pretty active here. I might have some bug spray in my bag."

He rifles through his backpack until he comes up with

a spray bottle. He hands it off to me, and I give my arms and legs a generous spritz. I don't know if it's going to help, but it smells terrible. I hand off the bottle to Noah, who gives his own arms a spritz. He was smart enough to wear jeans, at least. He tries to give the bottle to Warner, who waves it away.

"Mosquitoes never bite me," Warner says.

"Lucky," I mutter. "They *always* bite me."

Warner shifts on the ground. "It must be your blood type."

"My...blood type?"

He nods. "I have A-positive blood, which is not the preference of most mosquitoes." He looks me up and down. "What's your blood type?"

The itchiness on my arms ramps up a notch. Warner is making me uncomfortable. "I don't know."

"You don't *know*?" He looks at me like I've committed a deadly sin. "How could you not know your blood type?"

I shrug helplessly. "I...I just don't."

"Mine is AB-positive," Michelle volunteers. Thanks.

"It's very dangerous not to know your blood type, Claire." Warner's blue eyes are boring into me. "What if you were to get into a terrible accident and lose a lot of blood?"

"I..." There's a buzzing sound in my left ear. Another damn mosquito. "I don't know."

He shakes his head. "It could be a matter of life and death. For you not to know something like that..."

Before I can sputter out another excuse, Noah speaks up. "She's O-positive."

I blink at him in surprise. "Oh. How did you know that?"

He smiles crookedly. "I remember the doctor saying it when you were pregnant with Aidan."

I feel a sudden, surprising rush of affection for my husband. Of all the things he's forgotten over the years, including my birthday last year, I didn't expect him to remember my blood type. I suppose if I got into a terrible accident, he would have my back.

"That's why mosquitoes bite you so often," Warner says. "Mosquitoes love type-O blood."

Well, lucky me.

Jack is rifling around again in his backpack. "So we've got about a quarter of a bottle left of water," he announces. "If we finish it now, hopefully we'll be able to find water in the morning."

The thought of not being able to find water tomorrow is unthinkable. Part of me wonders if we should conserve some of our remaining water, but I'm *so* thirsty right now. And a quarter of a bottle split between five people isn't very much.

Jack pulls out the bottle with the remainder of our precious water. He lets Michelle take a few sips first, then drinks himself, then passes the bottle to Warner. There's hardly any left by the time it gets to Noah.

He glances over at me, takes a quick swig, then hands me the remainder. It doesn't look any emptier than it did when Warner finished with it.

"Did you get enough?" I ask Noah.

He nods. "I'm good."

Well, I'm certainly not going to force him to drink more. I tilt the bottle back and drain the remainder down my throat. The water tastes a little chalky, but I could drink a gallon of it at this point. It's almost painful to have to stop. I want to open it up and lick the inside.

I hand the empty bottle back to Jack. He tucks it away in his backpack. I hope to God we find water tomorrow morning. I don't want to think about what will happen if we don't.

I clear my throat. "Hey," I say. "I was just thinking, maybe we could all say our favorite memory about Lindsay."

The other four people around the fire could not possibly look less enthusiastic about this idea.

"Uh, sure," Jack says. "That sounds like it would be... nice."

I want to mouth the words "Thank you" to him, but I don't want to give any reason for Michelle to be more suspicious than she already is.

"Do you want to start, Claire?" Jack asks.

"Sure." I shift on the ground, trying to get comfortable in the dirt. I never sit cross-legged on the ground anymore. Not since kindergarten. "I guess my favorite Lindsay memory is from college. I had just found out my jerk boyfriend was cheating on me..."

"Noah?" Michelle asks. She sounds like she's teasing me, but there's also an edge to her voice. I'm sure she has an inkling that my marriage is a mess. It doesn't take a divorce lawyer to figure that one out.

"No. It was some other guy." I run a finger through the dirt next to me in the pattern of a star. "I dated him the year before Noah and I got together." I glance at Noah, but he's looking down at his muddy sneakers. "Anyway, when I got home, I was almost ready to start crying. So Lindsay suggested we break into the dorm kitchen, and we spent the night in there, baking and eating chocolate-chip cookies."

I don't tell them all the details from that night. Like the way Lindsay stroked my hair to make me feel better. Or how we made one cookie almost entirely out of chocolate chips. How we got caught in our caper by the heads of the dorm and Lindsay took all the blame.

I miss her so much already. I can't believe she's gone. I'll never forgive myself for letting this happen to her.

"Okay, I've got one." Jack pokes at the fire with a stick. "My favorite memory of Lindsay is the day I first met her. I was carrying this care package from my mom up to my room, and I saw this really beautiful girl on the stairs, and I got so flustered I dropped the whole thing and the box opened up. There were brownies everywhere!" He grins. "But the best part is that Lindsay and I ate the brownies off the stairs."

"Ew!" I laugh.

"That's all right." Jack pats his gut. "I've got a strong stomach." He squeezes Michelle. "How about you?"

Michelle frowns. "What?"

"What's your favorite Lindsay memory?" he asks.

"Oh." She shrugs. "I didn't know Lindsay very well."

"Yes, but you must remember something about her."

Michelle grits her teeth. She does not want to participate in this game. Truth be told, I don't think Michelle liked Lindsay any better than she liked me. And Lindsay didn't think much of Michelle. *She's so cold—like she doesn't have any real emotions,* Lindsay used to say.

"She had nice hair," Michelle finally says.

I shoot her a dirty look. Of course, if Lindsay is somewhere up there listening in, I don't think she would be unhappy with that memory. She would want to be remembered as having nice hair.

"I've got one," Noah speaks up.

His hazel eyes are staring into the fire, and there's a ghost of a smile on his lips. It makes me realize how infrequently I see Noah smile these days.

"So when I decided to propose to Claire," he says, "I asked for Lindsay's help picking out a ring."

"You did? I never knew that."

He grins. "Yeah, and you're lucky I did. You don't know what ring I would've picked out on my own." He shrugs. "Anyway, she helped me pick out the ring, and she even bargained for a better price. I mean, it was this fancy jewelry store, and somehow she was haggling with them. But it worked. I never would have gotten such a great ring without her."

"It was a really nice ring," I say softly. I never wear my engagement ring because it's too nice. I'm afraid I'm going to lose it or get mugged or something.

His eyes are distant. "And she made me review what I was going to do when I proposed. She insisted I had to get down on one knee, even though I thought it was cheesy. She was like, 'Noah, the one knee is *not* optional.'"

I find a smile touching my own lips. "I did love your proposal."

"Yeah, well." His eyes drop back down to his sneakers. "I really, really wanted you to say yes."

There was no way I wasn't going to say yes to Noah. We had graduated a couple of years earlier, and we were already living together. Even though we had been together since college, I was still so infatuated with him. He could've proposed to me with an *onion* ring and I would have said yes. But I loved that he got down on one knee in the middle of a nice restaurant and presented me with the most beautiful ring I had ever seen in my life.

"How about you, Warner?" Jack says.

Warner frowns. "I don't know. I don't have a favorite memory."

"You don't have *any* memories of Lindsay?" I say. That probably came out a bit more confrontational than I meant it to. "None at all?"

"Not really. Nothing that stands out."

Something about this man is really starting to irritate me. "But you were dating for six months. How could you not have any memories of her?"

"I have memories of her," Warner says patiently. "I just don't think any of them are worth mentioning."

I fold my arms across my chest. "She told me you were going to propose this week."

His mouth falls open. "She told you that?"

"She certainly did."

A smirk plays on his lips. "Well, I'm afraid she would have been very disappointed."

I blink at him. "She told me you hinted you were looking at rings."

"Yeah, well." Warner kicks at the dirt with the heel of his shoe. "Lindsay had a very vivid imagination, as I'm sure you know."

I want to jump off the ground and strangle Warner with my bare hands. My hands ball into fists, but before I can do anything stupid, I feel Noah's palm on my leg. I look over at him, and he shakes his head.

"Not worth it," he says under his breath.

He's right. What's the difference if Warner would have broken Lindsay's heart? There's nothing I can do about it at this point anyway. Better to let it go. After this week, I'll never see Warner again.

"I'm exhausted," Michelle announces. "Are we still reminiscing, or can we go to sleep?"

I want to be irritated at Michelle for her comment, but I have to admit, I'm tired too. I can't even keep my eyes open anymore. Everybody nods in agreement, and with the fire still going, we curl up on the uncomfortable forest ground to try to snatch a little bit of sleep. Michelle and Jack cuddle up together, and I feel a jab of jealousy. Noah and I are sleeping as far apart as we do in our bed at home.

The ground is not comfortable. That's an understatement. I never considered myself any sort of princess, but sleeping on dirt is not ideal—the leaves do nothing. A rock pokes me in the small of my back, and there's some sort of plant jabbing me in the shoulder blade. Every sharp edge in my body is suddenly in pain.

I turn onto my side, hoping that might be better. It isn't. I try my back again. That's probably the best position, but it's far from comfortable. I would give my little finger for a pillow or a blanket. Hell, I might give up two fingers for that.

Even so, I'm very tired. The sky is overcast, but I can still see the moon above. It's a full moon, and there's something almost hypnotic about it. My eyes start drifting closed. Until...

I hear a howl.

I sit up straight, suddenly wide awake. "Did you hear that?"

Michelle groans. "Oh my God, Claire, go to sleep!"

"Something howled." My heart is pounding as I look around. "Nobody else heard it?"

"I think you're hearing things again," Jack says.

My face burns. He's taking her side. Yes, she's his wife. But he doesn't love her. My relationship with Jack has been the only thing keeping me going for the last few months. It's really hard to see him all lovey-dovey with his wife, even if I know it's just an act.

Noah sits up, rubbing his eyes. "I heard it."

At that moment, I forgive him for all the toilet paper rolls he failed to change over the years. "You did?"

He nods. "It sounded like a wolf or coyote or something."

"It was probably just the wind," Jack insists. "But whatever it was, it's very far away. I wouldn't worry about it, especially with the fire going."

I scramble to my feet and look around us. For the most part, we're surrounded by trees, blocking my view of our surroundings. There could be a coyote ten feet away, licking its lips, and we would have no idea. There are small gaps between the trees, but there's no visibility. Especially not at night, with only the small fire and the moon illuminating the clearing. If only we had brought a flashlight.

I hear the howl once again. Is it getting louder?

I step over to one of the trees in the direction of the sound. I squint into the darkness. I can't see anything. I take another step, my heart thudding in my chest.

"Claire?" Noah says. "What are you doing?"

I take another step, listening for the rustling of leaves. Or the sound of an animal's footsteps growing closer.

Something brushes against my ankle. Something that feels like fur. I let out a screech and jump away. But when I look down at the ground, there's nothing there.

"Claire!" It's Jack's voice this time. "Stop worrying

about it. We're *fine*. The animals will leave us alone with the fire here."

I take a shaky breath. I suppose he's right. And even if it's not, what can we do? One of us could stay awake and be coyote watch all night, but I don't see any volunteers. I might volunteer, but my eyelids feel like lead.

"I'm sure it will be okay," Noah murmurs.

I nod and settle back down on my makeshift bed of leaves. There's not much we can do either way. I'll just have to hope for the best.

CHAPTER 17

ANONYMOUS

My dad taught me how to shoot in our backyard.

We had been planning a hunting trip for weeks—just me and him. It ended up later getting canceled because of an unexpected business trip to Toledo. But at the time, I thought we were going. And my dad said I had to know how to shoot if we were going hunting.

He set up a bunch of tin cans on a cardboard box. He said we were going to practice until I could shoot all of them. Our neighbors wouldn't mind. Most people in our town owned guns and were proud of it.

We stood in the grass together, eyeing the tin cans like they were wild animals. My Orioles baseball cap kept the sun out of my eyes. It was a straight shot.

"So here's what you do, sport," he said. "You keep your feet apart. Square your shoulders. Keep your right foot just out in front of your left." He helped adjust me until I was standing just right. "Good. Now you put the buttstock of the rifle near the centerline of your body and high on your chest."

He took a step back, examining my pose. "Elbows down."

I listened carefully, trying to do everything he told me. He showed me how to bring the rifle to my head and press my cheek firmly into the stock. Then he taught me how to aim.

"Good job," he said, and I flushed with pride. "Keep both your eyes open. Don't pull the trigger—squeeze it. You want constant pressure."

I took a deep breath. I aimed at the can farthest on the right and squeezed the trigger like he told me.

I missed by a mile.

"You gotta relax," he said. "You're too tense. Take a breath before you shoot. Then squeeze the trigger on the exhale."

I took a deep breath. I shot at the can again. I missed, but I came closer.

"Good job," he said. "Now try again."

I stared at the can. I imagined my mom's face in the center. I took a breath, then I squeezed the trigger. I heard the ping of the bullet penetrating the metal.

"Great!" He clapped me on the back. "You did it!"

We spent the next hour practicing shooting. I couldn't wait to go hunting with my dad. Just the two of us.

Finally, my mom came out into the backyard, her hands folded across her chest. She was wearing a tight blue sundress and had a face full of bright makeup. She smelled like flowers. When my dad was away, she wore sweatpants and undershirts. She didn't bathe for days.

"Haven't you been out here long enough?" she whined.

"A kid's got to know how to shoot," my father said.

She flashed me that same look she always gave me when my father paid more attention to me than he did to her. She wanted him to herself.

I still had the rifle in my hand. As I looked at my mother, I imagined a tin can where her face was. I had gotten to be a decent shot in the last hour. If I aimed the rifle at her, would I make the shot? I could always say it was an accident. I was a beginner, after all.

"Whoa, sport." My dad gently pried the rifle out of my hands. "You gotta be careful where you're aiming that thing. You don't want it to go off by accident."

I heard the sharp inhale of my mother's breath. She knew what I wanted to do. And if my father hadn't stopped me, I would've done it.

CHAPTER 18

CLAIRE

Morning arrives and I have not been eaten by a coyote. That said, I feel like shit. My head is throbbing from lack of water, and my mouth feels like it's stuffed with cotton. My arms and legs are heavy like I've got a weighted blanket on me. I slept through the entire night without tossing or turning, but somehow, I feel hungover.

I look over at Noah beside me. His brown hair is sticking straight up, and he's rubbing his eyes. When he pulls his hands away, there are purple circles under his eyes.

"Sleep okay?" I ask.

"I guess." He groans and rubs his temples. "I hope we can find the hotel quickly."

Warner is sitting across from us, also rubbing his eyes. He lets out a loud yawn. He's a little worse for wear as well, but he still could easily be on the cover of some wilderness fashion magazine.

I reach into my purse and pull out my cell phone,

hoping my reception miraculously returned overnight. Not only do I not have any service—not even one stupid bar—but my battery is at 1 percent.

I don't get it. According to the guys, we are less than a mile away from the hotel. How could there be no cell service whatsoever?

I'm sure Penny called last night so the kids could talk to us. What is Emma thinking? She must be terrified. I hope Penny made up a good story. When I didn't contact her last night, would Penny have called the police? Is there someone out there searching for us right now?

But no. Penny is not a worrier. Emma is the one who gets scared.

I feel this sudden, intense longing for my children. I want to gather them both in my arms and give them a giant hug. The feeling is so strong I have to cover my mouth to keep from crying.

What if I never see them again?

"Michelle!"

My head jerks up at the sound of Jack's voice in the distance. I suddenly realize he and Michelle aren't around the dead campfire anymore.

"Michelle!" Jack's voice calls out.

"What's going on?" I mumble.

Noah just shakes his head, and the two of us get to our feet. Every joint in my body screams in pain as I stand up, but after a few steps, the pain subsides to a dull ache. Jack is standing at the edge of the clearing, a wild look in his eyes. His hair is as disheveled as Noah's, and there's a rip in the sleeve of his T-shirt. He cups his hands around his mouth and yells, "Michelle!"

I clear my throat. "What's going on, Jack?"

He turns to look at me. His puppy-dog brown eyes are bloodshot. "I can't find Michelle."

"What?" Noah frowns. "What are you talking about?"

"I woke up and she was *gone.*" His eyes dart around like he expects her to pop out from a bush at any moment. "I don't even see any footprints. I don't get it. Where would she have gone?"

"She couldn't have gone far," I say. "She had a sprained ankle."

Jack rubs his fingertips against his temples. "I know."

"Maybe she went looking for water?" Noah says.

"Alone?" He shakes his head. "It doesn't make any sense. She wouldn't have gone off by herself. Not without me." He takes a deep breath, then yells out again: "MICHELLE!"

"Hey." It's Warner's voice coming from behind us. We turn to look at him. "I found footprints I think belong to her."

Sure enough, there is a single set of footprints leading off in a completely different direction. It's hard to tell who the footprints would belong to, but they seem about the size of a woman's sneaker. The footprints disappear into the trees.

It seems inconceivable to me that given her sprained ankle, Michelle would suddenly wander off by herself into the woods. But there's no other explanation.

"Should we follow them?" Noah asks.

Jack nods silently. But then he goes back to our camp and grabs his backpack. He unzips it and pulls out a pillowcase. He starts pulling parts of something black out of the pillowcase. I watch him for a moment before I realize what he's doing.

"You brought the rifle," I breathe.

"Yes." His voice is clipped. "I did."

"You told Michelle you didn't bring it."

He lifts his bloodshot eyes. "I lied."

It takes him a minute to assemble the pieces of the rifle. This whole thing is freaking me out. I had no idea Jack had a gun. Presumably, he only brought it for hunting. And maybe now that we're stuck out here in the woods, it's good that we have it.

But it makes me uneasy that he lied to Michelle and the rest of us about it.

Now that the gun is assembled, we all start down the path formed by Michelle's footprints. I don't hear any animal noises anymore, but it occurs to me that this is the same direction from where I heard the howling sound last night. What if she took a walk and ran into a wild animal?

The footprints continue for about ten yards before something catches my eye. Something white.

"Isn't that a piece of Michelle's shirt?"

There's a scrap of fabric hanging off one of the tree branches. Jack runs his finger along it and then yanks it off. "I think it's hers," he says.

He raises his gun, his eyes scanning the wilderness. My heart is thudding so loudly, I can't believe everyone else doesn't hear it. I look around the woods, expecting Michelle to jump out at any moment. But she doesn't. And then I see…

"Look!" I cry out.

Everybody looks down at where I'm pointing. There's a large rock behind one of the trees, and it's been drenched in something crimson. And that same color stains the grass all around it.

We creep closer. All that red. There's only one thing it could be. And the closer we get, the more obvious it becomes.

It's blood. And a lot of it.

"Oh, Christ." Jack lowers the rifle. He starts to sway and eventually collapses to his knees. "Oh my God."

"It might be blood from an animal," Noah says, although it's obvious he doesn't really think so.

I try to put a hand on Jack's shoulder, wanting to comfort him the way he comforted me after we lost Lindsay, but he roughly shrugs me off. I don't try again.

"Do you think an animal got her?" Warner asks. He doesn't seem particularly upset, simply curious. "Maybe she went to take a walk and that coyote Claire heard dragged her away."

"If she got attacked, she would've screamed." Jack's gaze settles on us one by one. "And if she had screamed, one of us would've heard her." He looks up at us. "Did anyone hear a scream during the night?"

We all shake our heads no. After I dozed off, I didn't hear a thing. I slept like the dead.

"How could you not have heard anything?" Jack's cheeks are pink. "It's impossible!"

"*You* didn't hear anything," Warner points out.

Jack makes a good point though. Something traumatic happened to Michelle, and it seems unlikely she wouldn't have made a sound. So how come none of us heard her?

And why would Michelle take a walk when she had a sprained ankle? Especially since she wasn't very comfortable in the woods. No, she would have stayed close to the camp.

None of this makes sense.

My stomach lets out a low growl. The last thing I ate was some of Jack's beef jerky last night, and now that we don't have water, I can't eat anything else salty. He also has some trail mix, but that's not much better. It's just salt on salt on salt.

Water—that's what I want. I would give up an entire hand for some water right now. Just thinking about it makes me dizzy.

As if reading my thoughts, Warner says, "We need to start looking for a water source."

Jack looks like he wants to strangle Warner with his bare hands. I know the feeling. "Michelle is *missing*. We have to find her."

"There's no point," Warner says. "Look at how much blood there is here. It's too late for her."

A terrible look comes over Jack's face. His fingers clutching the rifle turn bloodless. He stands up from the ground and points the rifle at Warner's chest.

The color drains from Warner's perfectly chiseled features as he takes a step back. "What the hell do you think you're doing?"

"Michelle is my wife," Jack hisses. "We are going to look for her. If she's hurt, we're going to find her. Do you understand me?"

I freeze, watching this impasse between the two men. I'm only peripherally aware of Noah grabbing my arm and pulling me back a few steps.

A muscle twitches in Warner's jaw. "I don't have a choice then, do I?"

"No." Jack doesn't lower the rifle. "You fucking don't."

Noah clears his throat. "Jack, we'll all look for Michelle. But you've got to put the gun down. Okay?"

Jack slowly lowers the rifle with shaking hands. For a moment, I'm certain Warner is going to make a grab for it, but he doesn't. Still, Jack has made an enemy. He needs to watch his back.

CHAPTER 19

CLAIRE

Michelle!" I call out. "MICHELLE!"

No answer. We've been looking for Michelle for the last thirty minutes. My voice is hoarse from calling out her name, coupled with the lack of water. Aside from that set of footprints and the blood on the ground, there are no other signs of Michelle. It's like she just vanished into thin air.

Now that the adrenaline has worn off, I'm starting to drag. I'm dizzy from lack of water, and the blisters on my feet are aching. I want to stop searching for Michelle and try to find water. Or better yet, keep looking for the inn.

"Michelle!" I call again.

I try to imagine the situation if things were reversed. Would Michelle be tromping around the woods looking for me? I highly doubt it. Would Noah even have insisted that they look for me the way Jack did? I don't even want to think about it.

I turn around and realize the others aren't near me. Up till now, one of the three of them has always been within eyeshot. But now I realize I'm entirely alone in the woods.

But I know where I am. The clearing is behind me.

Or is it in front of me?

My legs wobble beneath me. I'm not lost, am I? I mean, I know that *we* are lost, but at least before, I was part of a group. I don't want to be separated from the group. Especially with no food or water.

I rest my hand against the nearest tree to steady myself. That's when I notice the claw marks etched into the bark. The same as I saw yesterday. Five deep gashes.

Then I look at the tree next to that one. That tree also has deep gashes in the wood.

And at the base of the tree is more blood.

As I stare down at the blood, I feel this prickling sensation in the back of my neck. Like something is watching me.

Hunting me.

I whirl around. There's a bush about twenty feet in the distance. The bush shifts on its own accord, and I see a dark shadow within. And then a low growl.

Oh my God.

"Noah!" I scream. "NOAH!"

I'm not sure why I called for Noah rather than Jack. I would have thought my instinct would be to call for Jack. After all, *Jack* doesn't hate me. And he's the one with the Boy Scout experience. But when I opened my mouth, my husband's name was the one that came out.

I have to hand it to him—five seconds later, Noah tears through the branches next to me and he's by my side. It turns out I was never lost after all. Noah's eyes are wide. "What happened? What did you find?"

"There's more blood on that tree over there." I reach out a trembling hand to point. "Also, I…I saw something down there. Something moving."

Noah squints off into the distance. "Where?"

"That bush…all the way over there."

"What did you see?"

I chew on my lip. "I…I'm not entirely sure. It looked like a wild animal. Not a bear, but something bigger than a coyote."

Noah looks off in the direction I was pointing. "I don't see anything, Claire."

I don't mention the feeling I got, like something was watching me. Like something was *hunting* me. He would think I was being paranoid.

"I found more blood too." Noah winces. "I have to be honest…it doesn't look good for Michelle." He looks back over at the bush where I was pointing. "I hate to think some animal got to her, but…I don't know what else could have happened."

The bush isn't moving anymore, but I can't shake that uneasy feeling. "Where are Jack and Warner?"

Jack has a rifle—something that could protect us. And Warner has the map that could get us out of here. Not that I don't trust Noah, but if a wild animal came bounding out of that bush, there's not much he could do to protect me with his bare hands.

"I can't find them," Noah says. "Let's go wait back at the campsite." He glances around. "We shouldn't be wandering around out here, given the circumstances."

I nod in agreement. Noah puts a hand on my shoulder to gently lead me in the direction of the clearing, which wasn't where I thought it was at all. I have a terrible sense of direction. Without the others, I would be doomed.

Warner returns to the campsite about ten minutes after we do, looking impatient and irritable. We have to wait another twenty minutes for Jack to come back. His shoulders are sagging and he has purple circles under his eyes. He didn't find her. Aside from scattered droplets of blood here and there, there are no more signs of Michelle.

Where could she have gone?

Did she get up to stretch her legs in the middle of the night? Was she having trouble sleeping? And then ventured into the woods and an animal leaped out of nowhere? Was it the same animal I saw in that bush? The one that made the horrifying claw marks in the bark?

If Michelle had an encounter with the animal that made those claw marks, she's almost certainly dead.

I can't imagine it. It's inconceivable. But if she isn't dead, where is she?

"We need to get going," Warner announces. "We need to find water."

Jack's eyes immediately darken. He isn't ready to give up just yet. But before Jack can raise his rifle again, Noah holds up his hands. "He's right, Jack. We've got to have water or else we're all going to die."

"But we can't just *leave*." Jack kicks at the dirt beneath his feet. "We haven't found her yet."

"Jack, I just…" Noah shifts his weight between his feet. "I don't think we're going to find her, man. I don't know what happened. If an animal got her or… But she's not here."

Jack's shoulders sag as he takes in Noah's words. He looks like he's aged ten years in the last hour. Finally, he says, "Fine. Let's look for water. Then I want to keep looking for Michelle."

"Okay," Noah says, but Warner rolls his eyes.

For once, I agree with Warner.

CHAPTER 20

CLAIRE

Finding water turns out to be a difficult task. I had been hoping we'd locate some stream with fresh running water, but as we look, it becomes increasingly obvious that's not the case. Jack spots the footprints of what he believes to be a rabbit, and we follow them to what appears to be a small, shallow, very muddy pond.

Ordinarily, I would never drink water that looked like that. I wouldn't even want to put my hand in it.

"Is that safe to drink?" Noah asks.

"I brought a pack of tablets that are supposed to kill the bacteria in water." Jack lowers his backpack to the ground and lays the rifle down beside it. "And we can use the pillowcase to strain the dirt out of the water."

As a general rule, I don't like drinking anything that needs to have dirt strained from it first. But right now, I'm so thirsty that I would lap up the water, dirt and all.

Jack strains the water through the pillowcase into his water bottle. I take out Noah's empty water bottle from my purse, and we fill that one too. The water still looks decidedly murky, but even so, I'm devastated when Jack says we have to wait an hour to let the pill work before we can drink it.

For a moment, I imagine my daughter's face if she saw the water we had to drink. She's the kind of kid who freaks out if there's so much as a smudge on her plate. What would she think about drinking from a bottle of water that has *dirt* floating in it? Of course, Aidan would probably find the whole thing funny—I once caught him tasting dirt when he was about three years old.

Oh my God, I miss my children so much. I've got to get home to them. I'll do whatever it takes.

Jack put down the rifle next to his backpack, and Warner is eyeing it. The whole thing makes me uneasy. I don't love the fact that Jack brought a gun on this trip, but even more than that, I don't want Warner to have it.

"Jack," I say, "maybe you should dismantle the rifle."

At least my suggestion calls his attention to it. He places his hand protectively over the gun. "After what happened with Michelle, I feel more comfortable having it handy."

Except, what *did* happen with Michelle? We're assuming an animal got her, but nothing about this makes sense.

And maybe that's why Jack wants the gun handy.

Warner yanks the map from his pocket. "We need to get back on track. We need to find this place."

"I told you." Jack closes his fingers around the rifle. "We're not leaving without Michelle."

It surprises me how protective Jack has become about Michelle. The last time we were lying in bed together at his house, with Michelle slaving away at the office, he acted like their marriage was a sham. But he's genuinely terrified for her. And my chest aches when I think about the way they cuddled together last night.

Jack acted like it was over between him and Michelle. But maybe that was a lie. The best I can say is maybe he thought it was true when he said it.

Or maybe it was never true. Maybe it was just something he said to get me into bed. And maybe I'm not the first woman who fell for his lies.

"Look," Warner says, "if Michelle is injured somewhere, our best chance of helping her is to get to a phone and call the police. We obviously couldn't find her on our own."

Jack glares at Warner, his hand still on the gun. After a moment, he swears under his breath, then picks up the rifle and stomps off into the woods. I don't know where he went, but he couldn't plan on going far. He left behind his backpack and the water bottles.

Warner watches him walk off, then lets out a long sigh. He drops down onto a fallen tree and rubs his temples. For the first time since we've been out here in the woods, he looks exhausted. In this state, I'm not even sure the Sears catalog would find a place for him in its pages. He takes the hem of his shirt and wipes his lower face with it.

"Are you okay?" I ask him.

"It's hot," he mutters.

After that declaration, he rips his T-shirt off entirely, peeling it from his sweaty chest. And…

Whoa.

I take back what I said about the Sears catalog. *Any* catalog would be happy to have this guy on their cover page. He is *ripped*. And tan. You could sort of tell when he had his shirt on, but with it off, nothing is left to the imagination. I think there might be a little drool coming out of the corner of my mouth.

Lindsay is a lucky girl.

Was. Was lucky.

I flinch, remembering the future Lindsay had been imagining for the two of them. She really, really liked this guy—I'd never seen her so infatuated. And it wasn't just about his looks. She wasn't *that* superficial.

"Listen," I say. "When we get back, I thought maybe you could help plan the service for Lindsay."

I can't bring myself to say "memorial service." He knows what I mean.

Warner mops his face with his damp T-shirt. "That's all right. I mean, we were only dating a few months. The people who knew her best should be doing that."

"Yes, but I know that's what she would have wanted." I force a smile. "She really liked you."

"That's okay."

"But Lindsay would—"

"Look." Warner cuts me off before I can say another word. "I'm just trying to be polite here. I don't have the time to plan a big sad event for some girl I was going to break up with in a few weeks anyway." He grits his teeth. "I'm sure you've got plenty of time to plan this, between driving your kids to soccer practice and your yoga classes."

My mouth falls open. "I work full-time, you know. Just like you do."

Warner snorts. "As a *teacher*. I'm a *surgeon*, Claire. There's no comparison."

My face burns. I know he's upset about everything that's happened so far, and we're all thirsty and hot, but this guy is really showing his true colors right now. Sometimes hardship brings out the worst in people.

"Hey," Noah says sharply. "Claire works really hard at her job, you know."

I didn't expect him to stick up for me. I can't remember the last time he defended me. Usually I'm defending myself against *his* insults.

"I'm sure." Warner cracks his knuckles, and the sound resonates around us. "I'm sure babysitting a bunch of grade-schoolers all day is *life and death*."

Noah's face darkens, and his right hand balls into a fist. I take a step back, worried this conversation isn't going anywhere good. In all our years of marriage, I've never seen Noah throw a punch, and I have no idea if he would ever do something like that. But judging by all those muscles in Warner's chest, I'm not sure how well Noah would fare if it came down to it.

Fortunately, Jack bursts back out of the trees at that moment. His eyes are bloodshot and puffy. Was he crying just now? Is that why he left us?

"All right." His voice is shaky. "Let's go."

"Jack," I say gently. "Are you okay?"

"I'm fine," he snaps at me. "I said let's get going."

Apparently, he doesn't want to talk about it.

We still have a little while before the water is safe to drink, but we decide to get going. And now, of course, it's back to the same. Jack and Warner (with his shirt thankfully back on) looking at the map, then studying Jack's compass, then telling us what direction to walk in. I try to keep up with them at first, but then I end up hanging back like before. They walk faster than I do, and it's hard to keep up.

Unfortunately, this means I'm alone with my thoughts. Every time I shut my eyes for a moment, I think of Lindsay's pale body lying on the ground in the woods. I couldn't find her again if my life depended on it. I still feel sick that we left her there.

It's amazing how easily life can come to an end. Just a handful of berries, and that's it. Done. She's gone forever.

I could have eaten those berries. I'd be lying in the dirt next to Lindsay if that had happened. Noah told me he was glad I didn't eat the berries, but I can't imagine him crying if I died yesterday. The kids would care; my parents would care; Penny would care; but Noah? I don't know.

Well, I can't let myself think that way. I did survive. I got a second chance at life, and I don't want to blow it. I realize now what's important. Getting home and seeing my kids again. That's all that matters anymore.

I lift my eyes—the men have gotten way ahead of me. My heart jumps in my chest and I quicken my pace. I don't want to fall too far behind. I don't want to disappear like Michelle did.

At the end of the hour, we sit down and drink some of the muddy water. It tastes about how you would think it would taste. I gag slightly, but it's better than the alternative. We eat a bit more of Jack's beef jerky and some trail mix.

"How much more food do you have?" I ask him.

Jack rifles through his backpack. He looks a lot calmer than he did this morning, like his mini breakdown never happened. "If we conserve, maybe another day's worth."

Another day's worth. We've got to find the inn or at least *something* in that time, right? "And then what?"

"Well," Jack says thoughtfully, "there are some plants

here that we could safely eat. Also, I could try shooting a rabbit."

I clutch my chest. "You're going to kill a bunny?" Killing Thumper would be almost as bad as killing Bambi's mother.

"Alternatively," he says, "we could eat bugs."

I roll my eyes.

"I'm serious!" Jack doesn't crack a smile—he may really be serious. "There's nothing wrong with eating bugs. In other countries, people do it all the time. I don't know why bugs are so taboo in this country."

I make a face. "Because they're super disgusting?"

Warner smirks. "I don't think Claire is going to eat bugs."

"I can cook them," Jack says. "That will entirely change the taste. I mean, you wouldn't eat raw meat. Cooked insects are actually not too bad. I ate them a bunch of times in the Scouts."

I genuinely don't think he's teasing me. He think we're going to be lost long enough that we're going to have to cook and eat insects.

I don't understand how we're still lost. Warner has a map and Jack has a compass. Between the two of them, we should be able to find *something*. Jack was a freaking Boy Scout, as he has told us a million times before. Why is he unable to follow a simple map?

After the brief rest for sustenance, we get up and start walking again. But this time, Noah hangs back with me.

"Hey," he says. "Can I talk to you?" He glances up at the guys a few yards ahead of us. "Alone?"

"Okay," I say.

My heart speeds up. I touch Jack's sweatshirt, which is tied around my waist now that the sun is high in the sky. Is Noah going to tell me he knows all about me and Jack? I don't want to have that conversation right now. If he asks me, will I admit it? I don't know. I don't want to lie to him, but a revelation like that is going to make the next week very uncomfortable.

As soon as we get out of earshot of Jack and Warner, he lowers his voice several notches. "Something is wrong," he says.

"What do you mean?"

"I mean…" He glances up at the two of them, then back at me. "Warner's map. It doesn't make any sense. It's wrong. Nothing is where the map says it's supposed to be."

My breath catches in my throat. "Are you serious?"

"Yeah, and…" He shakes his head. "I looked at a map before we left for the trip, and I don't remember that fork in the road or anything from Warner's map. Also…" He squints over at the two men, then back at me. "I don't trust Jack's compass."

"You don't?"

"I know Jack is supposed to be Mr. Wilderness, Boy Scout, whatever, but I know the sun rises in the east, and that's not where the compass says east is."

"Oh."

"Also…" He takes a deep breath. "Claire, I think we're going around in circles."

"You…you do?"

He nods. "I recognize things I've seen before. Very specific things, like this gash I saw in a tree. And…and that squirrel." He points to a squirrel lying dead and rotting in the dirt. I have to admit, there is something familiar about it. I remember seeing that squirrel before. "I think that compass is taking us in circles."

I frown. This is the last thing I expected him to say. I thought he was going to accuse me of infidelity. This might be worse. "So...what are you saying?"

"I'm saying..." He takes off his glasses and wipes the lenses briefly on his shirt before sliding them back into place. "I don't trust them to find our way out of here. I think...I think we'd be better off on our own."

"We?" I cough. "You want me to come with you?"

He blinks at me behind his newly clean lenses. "Well, yeah. Of course I do. You're my wife."

But we hate each other. I don't say the words, but he must be thinking the same thing. We've hated each other for years now. And especially during the entire drive here.

Yet now that we're lost out here, he doesn't seem quite as angry at me anymore.

"I think I can find my way out of here." He glances behind him. "My dad used to sometimes take me hiking when I was a kid, so I know what to do."

I'm surprised by this revelation. Noah's father died when he was in college, before I met him. He rarely talks about him. "You never told me that."

He shrugs. "It was a long time ago. But I remember the map. These woods aren't that big. If we weren't going around in circles, we'd have hit civilization by now."

"You think so?"

Noah nods firmly. Granted, I've never thought of him as very good at outdoorsy stuff like hiking, but my husband is a very smart man. He's a physicist. He wouldn't make an assertion if he didn't feel confident it was true. He wouldn't want to go off on his own unless he believed he could find civilization.

He reaches for my hand. I let him take it. I can't even

remember the last time Noah held my hand. It's been years. I forgot how warm and big his hand always felt in mine.

"Trust me, Claire," he says. "I wouldn't let anything happen to you."

I want to believe him. I truly do. But Warner has the map and Jack has the compass. Oh, and Jack has the remainder of our food. Noah has nothing, except a partially full water bottle in my purse. And he doesn't even have sterilization tablets, so if I go with him, that's all the water we'll have to drink.

"I think we should all stay together," I say.

He shakes his head. "I don't think it's a good idea."

I pull my hand away from his. "Look, Jack does know the outdoors. We couldn't even have built that fire last night without him. I think if we go off on our own, we might get in big trouble. It...it scares me. I mean, look what happened to Michelle."

His eyes get cloudy. "What *did* happen to Michelle?"

"I don't know, but...she went off on her own and now..."

Noah scratches at his hair until it stands up even more. "Okay, fine. We'll all stay together."

"You're not leaving us?"

He shakes his head. "I wouldn't do that to you."

I'm surprised at the relief I feel that Noah isn't insisting on taking off on his own. If he really did want to leave, it would be a hard decision whether to go with him. It seems like the obvious choice to stay with Jack, but Noah is my husband. Maybe I've grown to hate him, but I trust him.

And maybe I don't hate him quite as much anymore.

CHAPTER 21

ANONYMOUS

My mother was waiting for me when I walked in the front door. "Strip," she instructed me.

I hung my head as I pulled off my Red Sox baseball hat, followed by my T-shirt, then my shorts. I left on my underwear and my socks. My mom scooped the clothing into a plastic bag, then, to my surprise, she tossed the whole thing into the fireplace, where they were quickly devoured in flames.

"What are you doing?" I shouted.

"They're all contaminated," she hissed at me.

"You can't just wash them?"

She glared at me. "Maybe if you washed yourself better, you wouldn't be covered in lice."

I should have been able to guess what she would do next, but it still came as a surprise when she whipped out the razor. I took a step back. "No," I said.

"If you don't hold still, half your scalp is coming off too."

In the end, I let her do it. My hair was already very short, only about half an inch from my skull, but it felt different to be shaved bald. My head felt cold.

She put me in the shower after that. She watched me bathe, cranking the heat up so high that my skin turned bright red. She didn't leave until she watched me soap myself up. Then she finally left. Maybe to burn the rest of my clothing.

After I finished showering, I looked at myself in the bathroom mirror. My scalp was so white. And round. I looked like an alien.

I went to my bed and lay down on the bare mattress, because the sheets had been stripped. I'm sure my mom meant for me to put on a new sheet, but I didn't feel like it. Snowball wandered into the room and peered up at me curiously. I reached out to stroke her white fur, hoping it might comfort me, and she hissed at me. Even though she was just a cat, my mother had taught her to hate me. Snowball would never be shorn like I was.

I wanted to wear a baseball cap to school the next day, but they weren't allowed in the school, so I had to take it off when I entered the building. As I walked into the room, everybody started laughing. A note had gone home in our backpacks yesterday that a child in the class had been diagnosed with lice. My shaved head made it obvious it was me.

Ever since the beginning of the year, Bryan McCormick had made my life miserable. As soon as recess started, he came up to me with his buddies, and I knew I was in for it. He got right in my face.

"We all knew it was you," Bryan said. "You're the one with the cooties."

I looked away. Tried to ignore him like my dad told me to.

"I bet they're all over your body too," he said.

I felt my face turning red.

He laughed. "I bet they're even in your mouth."

"Shut up, asshole," I mumbled under my breath.

He raised his eyebrows. "What did you just say to me, loser?"

I lifted my eyes. "You heard me."

"Yeah?" He took a step closer to me. "Well, maybe you should take it back."

He wanted to fight, and that was fine with me. My hands balled into fists. I was small, but I was strong. I pulled back my right arm.

CHAPTER 22

CLAIRE

A couple of hours later, we're still lost.

I'm beginning to wish I had trusted Noah and gone off with him. Maybe we would have found some sort of civilization by now. It couldn't possibly be worse.

Or could it?

We all look like people who have been wandering through the woods for the last day. The hair in my ponytail is sticking to the back of my neck, and I've got dirt ground into my shorts and shirt. All the guys have a day's worth of beard on their faces, and their clothes haven't fared much better than mine. Even Warner doesn't look so good, although *GQ* would probably still take him for a segment on "roughing it."

We come across another small pond. There are a couple of gray-colored birds drinking from the water, their beaks slurping up the liquid in a way that is starting to make me jealous. Warner nudges Jack. "You should try shooting one of them."

Jack frowns. "Shooting them?"

Warner bobs his head. "We've had nothing but trail mix and beef jerky to eat for the last twenty-four hours. We can make a fire and cook up those birds."

"Oh." Even though Jack was the one who wanted to go hunting, he doesn't look excited by the idea of shooting some birds. "I guess."

"No shit. Just shoot the damn things."

Jack hesitates, but he finally lifts his rifle. I take a step back, because I have no idea what sort of shot he is. I wasn't on board with the idea of going hunting, but I feel oddly dispassionate about the idea of shooting these birds. It's not quite as bad as shooting Bambi's mother. Although they probably have little birds waiting for them back in the nest. The babies are probably waiting for them to come home and regurgitate some worms into their mouths or something. They're probably getting hungry.

Ugh, I need to stop thinking about this before I start crying.

Jack aims the rifle, but his hands are shaking. He adjusts it several times, but I don't know how he could hit anything.

"Christ, you're shaking like an old man," Warner snorts. "Don't you know how to aim?"

"Just let me do this," Jack says tightly.

"You're just going to waste a bullet and scare them off." Warner holds out his hand. "Let me try."

Jack tightens his grip on the rifle. "Yeah, right."

Warner throws back his head and laughs. "What do you think? You think I'm going to steal it from you and shoot you?"

Jack narrows his eyes. "You said it, not me."

"Well, in that case…" Warner takes a step closer to Jack. "You better keep a close eye on that gun."

Noah and I exchange looks. The animosity between Jack and Warner seems to be escalating by the minute. I'm beginning to be sorry Jack brought that gun. I wonder if he feels the same way.

Jack aims again at the birds. His hands are slightly steadier this time, but he still misses both the birds. And the gunshot scares them off, just like Warner predicted. So much for a chicken dinner.

"You shoot like a girl," Warner says.

I should probably be offended by that comment, but I just feel uneasy. And also, I'm sure I shoot worse than anyone here.

"Also," Warner adds, "you can't navigate worth a damn. We would've found that inn yesterday if you weren't here giving us the wrong directions."

Jack's ears turn bright pink. "I can navigate just fine. Your map is wrong. You must've printed out the wrong one."

"Right." Warner snorts. "Blame it all on me. That's convenient."

I take another step back. Warner and Jack both look steamed. I wish Jack didn't have that gun. What if he turns it on Warner and shoots him? I don't want this trip to end with Jack going to jail.

"You guys need to calm down," Noah says. Instead of backing away like I am, he steps between them. "We're never going to get out of here if you keep fighting like this."

They both keep glaring at each other.

"Jack." Noah holds out his right hand. "I think you should give me the gun."

Jack is quiet for a moment. He and Noah have been friends for a long time. I know that he trusts Noah. Of course, Noah trusted *him,* and look what happened.

"Fine," Jack finally says. He places the rifle in Noah's outstretched hand. "Take it."

Noah accepts the rifle. He holds on to it with surprising ease considering I've never seen my husband hold a gun before. Of course, I never knew he went hiking when he was a kid. Maybe there's other stuff I don't know about him from his past.

"Let's get going," Noah says.

And we keep walking.

CHAPTER 23

CLAIRE

We're never going to get out of here.

We're going to run out of clean water. We're going to have to eat bugs. I'm never going to see my children again. We're going to die here in the forest and the animals will eat our bodies.

This is our second day of wandering around the forest. It's starting to get dark again. How is it possible that we have been looking for this place for over twenty-four hours and we still haven't found it? Maybe the inn never existed in the first place. That's the only explanation I can come up with.

I stop walking and dig around in my purse for my phone. Except it won't even turn on—the battery died. I'm guessing everybody else's phones are in similar condition. So even if we find a place where there's a signal, there's nothing I'll be able to do about it.

"Claire?" Noah slows to a halt beside me. "Are you okay?"

"Sort of. Not really." I swipe at my eyes with the back of my hand. "Do you still have any battery left on your phone?"

I hold my breath as he takes it out of his pocket. The screen is black, like mine. He shakes his head. "No. It died."

"Great," I mumble.

He glances at the others and lowers his voice. "I told you what I think we should do."

I nod. I can't think straight right now. I'm so hungry and thirsty.

"If we haven't found this place by tonight, I think we should ditch them," he says. "Are you with me?"

I try to swallow but my throat is too dry. "I'm just…" A tear escapes my right eye. "I'm afraid we're never going to make it home. I'm afraid we're never going to see the kids again."

"Claire…"

"Don't tell me I'm being silly," I hiss at him. "Lindsay isn't going to make it home. Michelle isn't going to make it home."

"I know. I *know*." He runs a shaky hand through his hair. "I'm scared too, okay? But…I'm going to do whatever I can to get us home. I *promise*."

He reaches out and takes my hand. Despite how awful I'm feeling, his palm against mine is comforting. I remember how, when we were dating, we would walk down the street holding hands. And Noah would turn to me and smile, and I would smile back because I was so happy to be with him.

Jack is a few paces ahead of us. He pauses to look at his compass and turns back to make sure we're following him. He sees me and Noah holding hands, then he does a double take.

"Jesus Christ!" Warner says.

Noah and I jog over to where the two guys have stopped short. I clasp a hand over my mouth—if there were anything in my belly, I would probably be sick.

It's a wolf. No, wait, it's probably a coyote, since there are no wolves in these parts, according to Jack. And it's dead. There are angry claw marks on its belly, and there's fresh blood all over the ground around the animal. The coyote's intestines are starting to bulge out of the gash.

"Whoa," Noah breathes. He's still holding Jack's rifle, and his fingers whiten around the barrel.

I stare down at the claw marks on the belly. They remind me so much of the claw marks I saw on those trees.

As horrible as it is to look down at this animal, all I can think to myself is that something killed it. And I don't want to be next.

"What kind of animal do you think did it?" Warner says.

Jack frowns. "Could have been a bear. Maybe the coyote provoked it. Threatened its babies."

"Do you think there's a bear around here?" My voice is shaking.

"I told you, Claire." Jack seems impatient. "A bear isn't just going to attack us. Not out of nowhere."

"It attacked this coyote," I point out.

"Yes, but we don't know why." He glances at Noah. "And anyway, we have a rifle to protect us."

For some reason, that doesn't make me feel that much better.

"As much as I enjoy staring at this dead animal,"

Warner says, "we really should keep moving. It's going to be dark soon."

Dark. Another night in the woods, sleeping on the cold, hard ground, with a mattress made of leaves, with mosquitoes feasting on my bare skin, and howling sounds in the distance. I can't take much more of this.

Noah throws his arm around my shoulders. He pulls me close and whispers in my ear, "I promise I will get you home."

I wish I could believe him.

CHAPTER 24

CLAIRE

We're spending another night in the woods.

At least by now, we know the drill. We find a clearing with even ground. We gather wood to put together a fire and collect leaves to form into makeshift beds. We did find a larger stream with less muddy water, so we've got enough to drink at least. But food supplies are extremely low. We'll have enough for breakfast in the morning, but then…

That's it.

What are we going to do if we run out of food? What if we starve to death in these woods? I know it takes a long time to starve, but it doesn't seem so ridiculous anymore. What if I don't make it home to Emma and Aidan? What will they do without me?

"If you could shoot, Jack, we'd have something more to eat," Warner grumbles as he goes off to collect twigs and branches.

Jack doesn't take the bait. Noah has been carrying

the gun the entire day. Somebody might be dead if he weren't.

Even though it's hot during the day, it grows very cold at night. My teeth are chattering even in Jack's sweatshirt. I stand in the clearing for a moment, hugging myself, wishing we had the fire going already. But there's no time to just stand around. We won't have a fire unless I help out.

"Hey." Jack grabs my arm as I try to go deeper into the woods to get the firewood. I didn't even realize he was behind me. "I need to talk to you, Claire."

I pause and turn to look at him. As I said, I've always found Jack's rugged good looks to be attractive. That shaggy hair, the crooked smile. It was so sexy when he was hammering away in my kitchen. The truth is I didn't just like him in college. I've had a tiny, harmless crush on him for the last fifteen years. But when Noah and I were happy together, it wasn't something I ever thought about.

Right now, I'm not sure how to feel. Back when we were at that gas station, all I could think about was kissing him. And spending the week with him in my private room. Now the idea of messing around with Jack is the last thing on my mind. All I can think about is getting home to my kids. I certainly have no interest in kissing him—if he tried, I would push him away.

But it quickly becomes clear Jack has no intention of kissing me right now either. "Something strange is going on," he says.

"What do you mean?"

"I mean"—he points up at the sky—"last night was overcast and I couldn't see the stars. But I can see all of them tonight. And I'm pretty sure that's Polaris right there."

I don't get it. Why is he giving me an astronomy lesson? "Oh. Okay."

He reaches into his pocket and pulls out the compass. "Polaris is dead north. But look where the compass points to north."

I look down at the compass. Not only is it not pointing north, but it's pointing in the opposite direction. The compass is wrong. It's the same thing Noah said.

"This is the first time you've noticed it's wrong?"

"That's the thing." He shakes his head. "It's not always wrong. Based on where the sun is, it was definitely right this morning. I'm starting to think…" He frowns. "I feel like we might be going in circles."

Again, it's the same thing Noah said. Panic mounts in my chest. This does not sound good. It's beginning to feel like we're never going to find our way out of these stupid woods. I'm never going to make it home.

"How could that be?" I say.

"The only thing I could think of"—he lowers his voice a notch—"is that Noah or Warner has a magnet."

"What?"

"A magnet would throw off the compass, because it works based on the earth's magnetic field." He looks down at the small circle in his hand. "If you have a stronger magnet, the compass won't work. And furthermore, it will change directions based on where the magnet is."

"And you think…" I take a few deep breaths. "You think that Noah or Warner has a magnet?"

"It's the only explanation that makes sense." He clears his throat. "Unless it's you."

My cheeks burn. He's joking. He's obviously joking,

but part of me thinks maybe he's not joking. "Why would somebody do that?"

He shrugs. "Who knows? Warner is nuts. I wouldn't put anything past him. Also…" He glances behind him. "Remember how I told him my friend Buddy was the medical director at the hospital where he works, St. Mary's?"

"Yes."

"And he said he knew Buddy?"

I shift between my feet. "I guess so."

"Well, the thing is"—his fingers claw at his scalp—"I got it wrong. My friend Buddy works at *St. Elizabeth's*. Not St. Mary's. So there's no way Warner would know him if he actually worked at St. Mary's."

My heart flutters in my chest. "What are you saying?"

"I think Warner lied to us about where he works." Jack folds his arms across his chest. "Who knows if he's even a doctor at all?"

"I…I don't know what to say." I bite my lip. "Maybe he just said he knew your friend to be nice."

"Don't be naïve, Claire." He lowers his voice another notch. "I'm going to ask Noah for my rifle back."

"You don't trust Noah?"

He's quiet for a moment. "I don't trust anyone right now."

Ouch.

"What about Michelle?" I blurt out.

"What about her?"

I drop my eyes. My sneakers were almost white at the beginning of this trip and now they're caked in dirt. You can't even tell what color they used to be. "It's just that you were super lovey-dovey with her. That surprised me. And when she disappeared, you were…"

"What are you saying, Claire?" He blinks at me. "Michelle is my *wife*. And she might be *dead* for all I know. Do you really think I acted inappropriately?"

"You told me your marriage was a sham." He said it so many times, the words are burned into my brain. "But it didn't look like a sham."

He frowns. "You're acting like Michelle deserved to have something bad happen to her."

"I never said—"

"You know," he interrupts me, "she's the only one who believed in me when I wanted to start my contracting business. If not for her, God knows what I'd be doing right now."

I let out a breath. "So you were lying to me all along?"

I expected Jack to get defensive, but instead, he narrows his eyes at me. "You have some nerve, Claire."

And that's when I realize the truth about my affair with Jack. It was all a lie. He never really wanted to end things with Michelle. He *loved* Michelle. He only told me what he thought I wanted to hear.

Jack isn't the man I thought he was. How could I have made such a terrible mistake? I can't believe it took nearly dying to realize it.

I pull his sweatshirt over my head. It's covered in dirt and sweat, but that's not why I don't want it anymore. "Here. Take this back."

He holds up his hands. "It's freezing out here. Keep the sweatshirt."

He's right. Goose bumps are forming all over my arms. But I'd rather be cold than put the sweatshirt back on. "No thanks."

"Claire…"

"I said I don't want it."

He takes the sweatshirt back, yanking it out of my hands roughly. "Fine. Suit yourself."

He stalks away from me, gripping the sweatshirt in his right hand. My teeth chatter as I watch him go.

CHAPTER 25

CLAIRE

Last night, there were five of us around the fire. Tonight, there are four.

We barely speak. Jack pokes at the fire with a stick to keep it going. The fire shoots off orange sparks, and the burnt-wood smell makes me long for toasted marshmallows. Or really anything that isn't beef jerky or trail mix.

I can't help but think about the broken compass in Jack's pocket. Is he right that somebody brought a magnet to throw off the direction? It would certainly explain why we're going around in circles.

But why would somebody do that?

Noah nudges my foot with his. "You look freezing, Claire."

"I'm f-fine."

Okay, my teeth might be chattering just a little bit.

He arches an eyebrow. "What happened to the sweat-shirt you were wearing?"

"I, uh…" I glance over at Jack, whose attention is on the fire. "I didn't need it anymore, so I gave it back."

"But you're cold."

I'm not as cold as I was before we got the fire going. The heat radiating off it warms my fingers and my feet, although my back still feels cold and I still have goose bumps all over my arms. "I'm okay."

Noah looks at me for a moment and then pulls off his hoodie sweatshirt. "Here, take mine."

"But then you won't have a sweatshirt!"

"I never get cold." He pats his gut. "I've got plenty of padding."

I don't know what he's talking about. I have at least as much padding as Noah does, probably more. But I accept his sweatshirt and drape it around me. Even though he hasn't used any in at least a day, it smells like his aftershave.

"Thanks," I say.

His eyes crinkle. "No problem. But you still look cold."

"Well," I say softly, "maybe you can warm me up."

"I could try."

He holds out his right arm, and I cuddle up against him. For the first time since we got out here, I feel warm and safe in his embrace. I can't remember the last time Noah held me like this. At least some of the tension of the day drains out of me.

"Do you remember when Aidan was six months old and the power went out?" he asks softly.

I allow myself a smile. "Yeah. It was so cold in the house. The three of us all snuggled under a blanket, trying to keep warm together."

Noah squeezes me tighter. I miss the kids desperately,

but until now, I hadn't realized how much I missed my husband. The way he used to be. The way *we* used to be.

"God damn it, Jack!" Warner's voice interrupts my thoughts. "Will you stop poking the fire?"

"Do you want the fire to go out?" Jack turns to stare at Warner. "Will you get it going again if it does?"

Warner rolls his eyes. "Quit being a drama queen."

Jack is quiet for a moment as he pokes the fire. "We should've kept looking for Michelle."

Warner groans. "Not this again."

"None of you cared enough about her to keep looking." In the light of the fire, Jack's cheeks turn pink. "You all just left her. None of you cared."

"That's not true," Noah says quietly.

Jack snorts. "Please. You all hated Michelle."

I feel my face burn. I did hate Michelle. I remember the first time I met her, when Jack brought her out for dinner with me and Noah. Most of Jack's girlfriends before her were these sweet, fun, bubbly girls, so Michelle came as a shock. She was a little older, for one thing. And she was so serious and composed—her jet-black hair was pulled into an elaborate French twist and she wore a tasteful white blouse and pencil skirt. The other thing that surprised me about Michelle was she didn't hang on Jack's every word like the others. In fact, it was very much the opposite. Every time she opened her mouth, he stared at her like she was a celebrity.

Near the end of the meal, Michelle excused herself to go to the bathroom, leaving us alone with Jack. I had to go to the bathroom too, but I wasn't excited about being alone with Michelle. In that sense, not much changed over the years.

Isn't she great? Jack asked eagerly while she was gone.

Noah and I exchanged a meaningful look. *Great*, he echoed.

Of course, we could never tell Jack we thought Michelle was wrong for him. But we couldn't wait for them to be done.

But they never were done. All of a sudden, they were getting married, even though Jack always swore he didn't want to get married until he was at least forty. It wasn't all bad though. Thanks to Michelle's lucrative practice, they could afford a lifestyle that Jack never could have paid for on his own.

"I didn't hate Michelle," I lie.

"Me neither," Noah says. I suppose it's less of a lie in his case. He never really had a reason to hate her.

Warner shrugs. "I didn't even know her."

"Exactly!" Jack's hand balls into a fist. "*None* of you knew her. You didn't care about her. If you knew her, you never would've left her."

"Don't look at me," I say. "I didn't even want to leave Lindsay, remember?"

"Lindsay was dead!" Jack snaps. "There was nothing we could do! This was completely different!"

I've never seen Jack this upset before. Noah's arm tightens around me.

"Don't kid yourself," Warner says. "Michelle is dead too. She was supposed to be this brilliant lawyer, but she was too stupid to know not to go on a walk alone. And some wild animal killed her."

Jack's face is almost purple. "You take that back."

"I won't take it back. It's true." Warner shrugs. "At least I accept that my girlfriend is dead. You're in denial."

Jack scrambles to his feet. Before I even know what he's doing, I see him bend down and reach for something next to Noah. It takes me a second to recognize he's going for the gun.

But Noah is too fast for him. He places his hand protectively over the rifle. "Don't do this, Jack."

"Give me the gun, Noah."

"Not a chance."

"Give me the fucking gun, Noah!"

But Noah just shakes his head.

There's a tense moment when I'm scared Jack might fight him for it. What if one of them got shot out here? What would we do? Warner is a doctor, but he couldn't save Lindsay. If one of us got a bad gunshot wound, that would be the end.

"I'm gonna take a walk," Jack finally says.

Noah nods. "Good idea."

Jack takes one last look at the gun, then stomps off into the woods. I watch him disappear between two trees, not sure whether I'm scared or hoping he won't return.

"Your friend is a real nut job," Warner mutters.

I would have thought Noah would say something to defend his best friend, but he keeps his mouth shut.

"And you know what else?" Warner frowns. "That Michelle seemed like a real class-A bitch. Not that I got to know her or anything, but you can just tell."

"Not really." Noah lifts a shoulder. "She wasn't so bad. She just…she and Jack had issues."

I look at Noah, surprised he would defend Michelle, considering he never particularly liked her. But then again, if he really thinks she's dead, there's no reason to trash-talk her.

"Tomorrow we need to go north," Warner says. "We should use the sun to guide us, not that broken compass that's been taking us around in circles. The inn is north. I know that. If we go north, we're going to hit something."

Noah nods. "I agree."

For the first time all day, I feel a twinge of hope. The compass was obviously our problem. If we follow the sun, we will get to the inn.

"I'm going to try to get some sleep," Warner announces. "I've never been so tired in my whole damn life."

"Me too," I say. I let out a yawn as an almost painfully sleepy feeling comes over me. My eyelids feel heavy. It must be from all the walking. "I can't keep my eyes open."

I look over at Noah, wondering what's going to happen next. Last night, there was no question about whether we would sleep next to each other—we slept apart, as always. But now something has changed. I want him next to me. I want his arms around me while we drift off.

I lie down in my makeshift bed of leaves. Noah hesitates for a moment, then lies down right beside me. He drapes his arm around me, pulling me close to his body. Despite everything going on right now, a feeling of peace comes over me. I missed this so much.

I love you. The words are on the tip of my tongue. I haven't said that to Noah in so long. We used to say it all the time. It used to be how we ended every phone call. We never say it anymore. This is the first time in years that I feel the urge. The only thing stopping me is Warner lying a few feet away from us.

Noah pulls me closer to his warm body. The fire fades

away as my eyes drift shut. I'm so tired. I feel like I could sleep for days.

And I do sleep for a very long time. The only thing that finally wakes me up is the sound of gunshots.

CHAPTER 26

ANONYMOUS

The rules in our house were very strict.

Dinner was six o'clock sharp every night—you clean your plate or else. Come straight home immediately after school. Church every Sunday morning. Half an hour of television, only on weekends, and no TV at all if any rules were broken. And every night before bed, my mother would watch me say my prayers:

Now I lay me down to sleep.
I pray the Lord my soul to keep.
If I should live another day,
I pray the Lord to guide my way.
Amen.

If the rules were broken, there were consequences. When my dad was in town, it was usually something reasonable. No dessert. Go to bed early. But if he wasn't around, the punishments were more creative.

As I was coming home one day when I was twelve years old, my mom caught me chewing gum. We had recently moved to a new school, and I was trying hard to make friends this time. One of those friends had given me a piece of gum at school, and I chewed it all the way home. I had meant to dispose of the evidence once I got home, but my mom was vacuuming in the living room and caught me.

"What do you think you're doing?" she hissed at me.

I should have just spit it out and apologized. But I was dumb. "All the other kids at school are allowed to chew gum."

"You mean all your hoodlum friends?"

"It isn't fair," I mumbled under my breath.

"Fair?" My mom pushed the vacuum aside, her eyes flashing. "You want to talk about what's fair? Do you think it's fair that I'm stuck here with you while your father is off…"

I didn't say anything else. It was time to shut up.

"Gum." My mom held out her hand in front of my lips. I spit the flavorless gum into her palm. "Good. Now go outside and ask God's forgiveness for what you've done."

"Outside?"

It was January. One of the coldest days of the year. I had just walked half an hour to get home, and I could barely feel my toes in my sneakers. I didn't want to go back outside.

"Yes." She glared at me. "I'm not letting you up to your room with all your games and books. Outside. Now."

"But—"

"If you want to argue, I'd be happy to take your coat for you."

I had no doubt she would do it.

I trudged out to the backyard. It was even colder back there than it was on the street. Some of our neighbors had tire swings or play sets out in the backyard, but I had nothing. Not even a bike. The backyard was all just my mom's berry bushes.

I was hungry, but the bushes were barren right now. I hugged my chest, trying to keep warm. I jogged in place, which helped a little, but it didn't make my fingers, my toes, or my ears feel less frozen.

I walked over to the tiny wooden cross in the center of the yard. That was where Snowball was buried after she died the previous year. My mother had wept on her knees. I wondered if she would cry that way if something happened to me. I couldn't imagine it.

I waited and waited. After fifteen minutes, I was sure she was going to call me back in. But she didn't. The sun went down, and I was still out there. Waiting.

I was out there for three hours. She finally let me in for dinner. By then, my fingers and toes and the tips of my ears were bright pink and I couldn't feel them. I was scared I had frostbite and needed to see a doctor. I once read a story about a man who got frostbite when he was lost in a blizzard, and they had to remove part of his nose.

I ran my fingers under warm water but the feeling wouldn't come back. My mom watched me, clucking her tongue impatiently. She still towered over me—I was the shortest kid in my class. Most people thought I was three or four years younger than I was.

"I told you it's dinner time," she said. "If you don't want to participate, you can go back outside."

"I can't feel my fingers." I tried to make a fist with

my right hand. They moved but slower than I wanted. "I need a doctor."

She snorted. "Don't be ridiculous. Just eat your dinner."

"What's for dinner?" I asked.

"Do you think I'm your servant?" She blinked at me. "You can make your own food, can't you?"

I shouldn't have been surprised. When my dad was around, we ate well. His favorite meal was pork chops with apple sauce. He also liked my mom's lasagna. But when he wasn't around, I usually had to fend for myself.

I backed away from the sink and went to the refrigerator. My mom would not let me use the stove, so my choices were limited. I pulled out a loaf of bread and some peanut butter. My fingers were clumsy, but I managed to make myself a peanut butter sandwich. I only dropped the knife twice.

The next day, there were blisters on my hands and feet. When I went to school, I hoped my teacher would notice and send me to the school nurse so I could be seen without getting in trouble. But nobody noticed. No surprise there—my teacher had spider veins all over her nose and smelled like alcohol in the morning.

My fingers ended up okay after all though. I got feeling back and the blisters healed. You can't even see where they were anymore.

Two days later, when I pulled my favorite T-shirt out of my dresser drawer, I discovered there was a piece of chewed-up gum stuck to the shirt that had been there for days. I couldn't get it off.

CHAPTER 27

CLAIRE

What was that?"

I sit up straight on the ground, my heart pounding. The sun is just starting to peek up over the horizon, bright enough that I can see Noah still asleep beside me. But when I look up across the dead embers of our fire from last night, I discover the other two members of our party are gone.

"Noah." I shake his shoulder. "Wake up."

Noah groans and rubs his eyes with the balls of his hands. Like me, he's been wearing the same clothes for the last two days, and now he's getting closer to a full-on beard. "What? What's wrong?"

"I heard a gunshot." I hug my knees to my chest. "And Jack and Warner…they're gone."

"A gunshot?" Noah frowns. "But I've got the…" His hand goes to his side and touches only empty dirt. "Shit."

I squeeze my hands together. I definitely heard a gunshot. But I don't know where it came from. Where are Jack and Warner? And which one of them has the gun?

There's a rustling sound that comes from the wilderness to our right. Noah and I exchange looks. I swallow. "Should we…go look for them?"

He shakes his head. "I'll go check it out. You stay here."

"No way." I shiver inside Noah's hoodie sweatshirt. "I'm not staying behind."

"Claire…"

"If you're going, I'm going."

"Fine," he sighs. "But just…stay behind me."

We stand up, brush the dirt off our clothing as best we can, and move in the direction of the rustling noise. Even though we're hoping to find Jack or Warner, it doesn't mean they're the ones making the noises. It could be a wild animal. We could be walking into a very dangerous situation.

The woods are relatively quiet except for the sound of some birds chirping. I keep my eyes ahead of me but keep checking the ground to make sure I don't trip like Michelle did. If I twist my ankle, what will happen to me? Will they leave me behind? I don't think Noah would do that, but I don't want to find out.

Noah pushes his glasses up his nose as he peers into the distance. "I see somebody."

"Who?"

"I think…it's Jack."

I try to see over Noah's shoulder, but he holds up his hand to keep me behind him. I squint into the distance and can just barely make out Jack's silhouette. It's a relief. At least he's still alive.

"Jack!" Noah yells.

For a moment, we are met with only silence. But then the Jack-like silhouette turns in our direction. It's him. And he's got the rifle in his hand.

And Warner is nowhere to be seen.

"Jack!" Noah calls one more time as he waves his hand.

Jack waves back. He starts back in our direction, limping slightly on the uneven ground. I'm limping too. My feet are one big mess of blisters. I'm afraid to even look.

It isn't until Jack gets closer that I notice the crimson stains.

The knees of his jeans are dark red. His hands are stained as well. It's probably too much to hope for that he fell on a raspberry bush or something. There's only one thing those stains could be.

"Jack," Noah gasps. He takes a step back. "You… What is that on your hands and your pants?"

Jack holds out his hands, which are also stained with the same red color. "It's not what you think."

"Where is Warner?" I ask.

Jack shakes his head. "I don't know."

I swallow and look at the rifle in his hand. "I heard a gunshot."

Jack is quiet for a moment. Finally, he sits down on the ground and puts his head on his knees. I hear him mumbling something under his breath.

"Jack"—Noah drops a hand onto his shoulder— "what happened?"

He lifts his head. "I'm sorry I took the rifle back, Noah. I only did it because Warner disappeared and I wanted to go look for him. I mean, I don't give a shit what he does, but he's got the map. So…"

176

"Did you shoot him?" I blurt out.

Jack's mouth drops open. "No! Of course not. How could you think that?"

Um, because he's holding a rifle, I heard a gunshot, and he's covered in blood? I exchange looks with Noah.

Jack runs a shaking hand through his hair. "Yeah, I did shoot the gun. But only because I thought I saw a coyote."

"Don't they travel in packs?" I ask.

"Not always," Jack mumbles. "Anyway, the animal ran off after I shot the gun. But then I slipped on something wet all over the ground. It was…" He looks down at the dark red stains on his hands. "It's just like when Michelle disappeared."

Noah's face turns a shade paler, but I can tell he's trying not to let on that he's shaken. I, on the other hand, feel like I'm going to retch.

"It might not be Warner's blood," Noah says. "Maybe it's an animal."

"Maybe," Jack mumbles.

Noah looks off in the direction Jack came from. "Can you show us?"

I don't want to see a big pool of blood. But if we have any chance of finding Warner, we have to know what we're dealing with. And I'm not about to stay behind while the guys go off in the distance. So I grudgingly follow Jack as he takes us to the spot where he found the blood.

He wasn't kidding. There's a *lot* of blood all over the ground—even worse than yesterday. Crimson droplets are staining every blade of grass. There's no doubt what it is.

Then I look up at the tree nearest to us. There are five deep gashes in the wood. Like claw marks.

I close my eyes and try to imagine what could have made all this blood on the ground. Is it Warner's blood? If so, what happened to him? Did the coyote Jack saw get the better of him and then drag him away?

But it couldn't have been a coyote. A coyote would be too small to carry off someone as large as Warner. And it wouldn't leave those huge claw marks in the tree. If an animal did this to Warner, it would have been something much larger than a coyote.

I can't help but remember Emma's words when she begged me not to go on a trip. *I had a dream that a monster ate you.*

I wish I had listened to my daughter. A lump rises in my throat. I hope I get to see her again.

Jack is staring down at the puddle of blood, that distant look still in his eyes. There's another possibility, of course. I heard a gunshot. Maybe Jack wasn't shooting at a coyote. Maybe Jack shot Warner.

If he did, he had just enough time to hide the body between the gunshot and when we found him.

"We should look for Warner," Noah says. "If an animal attacked him, he might be lying somewhere, badly hurt."

"Right," Jack says, but there's no conviction in his words. I know how he feels. We didn't find Michelle yesterday, and I don't believe we're going to find Warner now. It's a waste of our time and energy. We need to focus on finding help.

Whatever happened to Michelle has now happened to Warner. He's gone. And we may never know what happened to him.

CHAPTER 28

CLAIRE

We spend an hour looking for Warner. Really, we're looking for the map. If we found that lying in the dirt somewhere, we would probably call off the search immediately.

I stay near Noah the whole time. The thought of getting lost on my own is too horrible to comprehend. Jack goes off on his own, but all three of us stay close to the camp we made.

"Warner!" Noah yells. He's called out his name so many times his voice is getting hoarse. The lack of water doesn't help. "Warner!"

No answer.

"Jesus," Noah mutters as he drops into a sitting position on a large rock. He wipes a bead of sweat from his forehead. "It's getting hot, isn't it? I don't think he's out there. We should find Jack and get going."

"Yeah."

The sun has risen in the sky, telling us which way

is east. We can figure out north and start moving in the direction of the inn. We may not have the map, but we're bound to hit something.

"Noah?" I say.

"Uh-huh?"

"Do you…" I clear my throat and cough. "Do you think Jack is telling the truth about shooting at the coyote?"

Noah blinks up at me. "Are you asking me if I think Jack killed Warner?"

"No."

He's quiet for a moment, looking up at the sky. "Listen, I know Jack and Michelle were acting lovey-dovey the other day, but he wanted out of that marriage. Badly."

I cough into my hand. "He did?"

Noah nods solemnly. "He was miserable. He kept telling me he didn't know what she was like when he married her. He knew he made a mistake. Also, he was…you know, cheating on her. And not just once."

I avert my eyes. "Oh, I…I didn't realize."

"Yeah." He lets out a sigh. "But what could he do? She's the best divorce lawyer in the state. He didn't want to lose everything."

I cover my mouth. "What are you saying, Noah?"

He glances around us. "I'm not saying anything. I just think this whole setup was sort of convenient. He packs this rifle. Michelle gets lost in the woods, even though she had a sprained ankle. I mean, if Michelle disappeared forever, it's not like it would be a bad thing for him."

"But what about Warner?"

Noah takes a deep breath and lowers his voice. "Warner told me something yesterday. I think you should know."

My legs suddenly feel like Jell-O. Whatever he's about to say, I'm not sure I want to hear it.

"The night Michelle disappeared," Noah says, "Warner saw Jack go into the forest with Michelle."

"*What?*"

I think I'm choking. I lower myself onto my knees on the ground. I feel dizzy. What Noah is saying couldn't possibly be true. Yet…

Jack did want out of his marriage. That's a fact. Despite our conversation yesterday, I don't believe he was lying about that. He told me once he felt sick at the thought of being married to "that woman" for the next thirty years.

Sometimes I think it would be worth it. To lose everything just to get rid of her.

Maybe this trip was his clever way of doing exactly that. And maybe he knew Warner saw him and he had to get rid of him too. And it *is* all awfully convenient for him. Here we are, lost in the woods thanks to Jack's faulty compass. It would be so easy for an animal to do away with one of us. Or more than one of us.

And what about Lindsay? She ate those berries, and it seemed like an act of God at the time. But Jack knows the woods better than anyone. Maybe he was hoping Michelle might eat the poison berries.

We started this trip with six of us. Now only three are left.

Maybe Noah or I will be next.

"Do you really think Jack killed them?" I whisper.

Noah avoids my eyes. "I…I don't know. I've known Jack since we were eighteen, and… No, I don't think he would do that. He's not a bad person."

Would Noah say Jack wasn't a bad person if he knew Jack slept with his wife?

If Noah suggested taking off now, just the two of us, I would be very tempted. But it seems cruel at this point to leave Jack behind. Of course, he's the one with the rifle.

"Anyway"—Noah shakes his head—"we better get going. I'm sure we're just letting our imaginations run wild."

Noah gets up off the rock and I follow him. But as I walk back to the campsite, I can't shake the horrible feeling that I might not make it home from this trip alive.

CHAPTER 29

CLAIRE

We walk due north, guided by the sun. We're not even attempting to use Jack's compass anymore.

The map is gone. Even though Noah said the map was wrong, I can tell both of them are uneasy navigating without it. We are walking forward into the unknown. We're just hoping we find something before we collapse.

The food is gone. We finished the last of it before we set off. And now I'm getting hungry, but I'm afraid to even think about what the options are. If Jack tells me we have to eat bugs, I think I'd rather starve. But I might feel differently by tonight.

We find a small stream and fill up the water bottles. Fortunately, the stream isn't too muddy, so we don't have to filter the water through a shirt. I watch it swirl around inside Jack's water bottle and I practically salivate.

"So I've got some bad news," Jack says.

Bad news? We've been trapped out in the woods for

two days. We don't have any food left. How much worse could it possibly get?

"This is my last purifying tablet." Jack drops the tablet into the water bottle. "So we really need to ration this."

My stomach sinks. This is pretty bad news. How long can a person live without water?

Noah puts his arm around me, but it doesn't do anything for the feeling of dread in the pit of my stomach. "It's going to be okay," he murmurs in my ear.

How is it going to be okay? *How?*

We all take measured sips from the water bottle, and Jack puts it back in his bag. As we start walking again, I wonder if Penny has contacted anybody about us. Surely by now she knows something must be wrong. We would never have gone two days without calling to speak to the kids. I'm sure Emma is freaking out.

Penny knows the name of the inn. She could call them and find out we never checked in. There could be a search party looking for us right now.

I squeeze my eyes shut. I just have to hang on to that hope. Somebody is surely looking for us by now. I have to get through this. I have to get back home to Emma and Aidan.

"Look!" Jack's voice interrupts my tortured thoughts. "Up ahead!"

If it's another coyote, I don't want to know.

I open my eyes. And my jaw drops open.

It's a cabin. About a quarter of a mile away. I can just barely see it, but it's real. And it doesn't look abandoned either. At the very least, we can go inside and get supplies.

"Oh my God," Noah breathes.

For the last hour or so, the three of us have been

chugging along slowly, but now we all get a burst of energy. We practically sprint over to the cabin. I feel like there's a chance it's a mirage and will disappear when we get too close. But it doesn't disappear.

It's real. We're saved.

As relieved and happy as I am to see the cabin, I get this uneasy feeling as we come closer. This is a lone cabin in the middle of nowhere. What sort of person would live out here? What if it's somebody who is violent or mentally ill? Jack has the rifle, but it doesn't make me feel that much better.

The cabin is small—only one story, probably only one or two rooms. The wood is old and splintered, and it's rotting away in patches. There are no lights on inside the cabin, but that doesn't mean nobody's home. Maybe it doesn't have electricity. Jack raps on the door, and we wait. Then he knocks again.

Noah walks around the side and looks through one of the windows. "I don't think anyone is home," he says. "I don't see movement inside, and there's no vehicle around."

"It might be a cabin somebody just uses for vacations." Jack clears his throat. "I think we should break in. It's an emergency."

He looks at us for confirmation. We both nod vigorously. There's no way I'm walking away from this cabin.

"Noah, check if the window is open," Jack says, but right as the words come out, he puts his hand on the doorknob and it turns. Looks like we won't have to break in after all. "Well, that was easy."

A little too easy. That terrible feeling in my stomach returns.

"Wait." I grab Jack's arm as he starts to go inside. "We need to be careful. What if somebody is lying in wait for us?"

"Lying in wait?" Jack's eyebrows shoot up. "Claire, the cabin is empty. There's no light inside, and there are no cars here. Nobody is inside."

I hold my breath as he pushes the door open.

CHAPTER 30

ANONYMOUS

My parents argued a lot at night.

I would hear them from my bedroom. My room was right above the staircase, so I could make out nearly every word. Mostly it was that my mom wanted my dad to stay home more. Stop traveling so much. I couldn't blame her, because that was what I wanted too.

When I was sixteen, they had one of the worst arguments I ever heard. They weren't even trying to keep their voices down.

"It's bad enough you're always leaving us to spend time with your floozies," my mother shouted at him. "You're always off having fun and I'm stuck here all alone."

"You're not alone," he pointed out.

She snorted. "I'd rather be alone."

"Don't say that."

My dad was the only one who ever defended me. Nobody else liked me. I hardly had any friends at school. Teachers complained I never participated in class and wouldn't look them in the eyes. And my mom hated me.

"But this is lower than low," my mom ranted on. "My own sister! How could you?"

"I'm not—"

"Liar!" There was a crash. My mom must've thrown something at him. "You tell her it's over right now!"

"Helen…stop acting crazy."

"Don't tell me not to act crazy, you cheating asshole!" Another resounding crash, followed by shattering glass. "Get out of my house!"

"Fine!"

I winced as the door slammed shut. It wasn't the first time he had stormed out, but each time, I thought it might be the last. I couldn't figure out why he ever came back. My mom was an awful person—she was always accusing him of terrible things. Maybe he was sticking around for me.

But eventually, she would drive him away.

I stared up at the cracks in the ceiling of my dark bedroom. I hated my mother. She was driving away the only person who gave a damn about me. If I didn't do something, he was going to leave. Forever.

I thought about my father's rifle. He kept it under the bed in the spare bedroom. What if I took it out and assembled it in the way he showed me? I could say I heard an intruder. Then my mom came out and I shot her by accident. What a tragedy.

Everyone would believe me. After all, why would I purposely shoot my own mother?

Could I do it though? I had shot at animals before but never a person. Much less my mom. If it came down to it, would I be able to squeeze the trigger?

But that was the wrong question. If I had a gun in my hand and my mother was standing in front of me, I wouldn't be able to stop myself.

As soon as the house was quiet, I crept out of my bedroom. I carefully made my way down the hall to the spare bedroom. My heart was beating very fast, but at the same time, I felt good. Really good. I didn't realize how much I wanted to do this.

The spare bedroom was dark and the double bed was made up. I crouched down next to the bed and felt around until my fingers grazed the metal case. Bingo. I yanked it out from under the bed, my hands tingling in anticipation.

Until I saw the padlock on the gun case.

I cursed under my breath. No swearing was allowed in our home, but I learned at school. Anyway, I wasn't going to be able to get to the rifle. So much for that plan.

I shoved the case back under the bed. My stomach growled loudly. I didn't have enough for dinner. My mom made only a small portion of chicken, so I had about a quarter of what everyone else had. I was starving. If I'd told her how hungry I still was, she would have yelled at me that I was ungrateful. But now that she was in bed, I could go down to the refrigerator and sneak a snack.

I crept down the stairs to the kitchen. Our staircase was creaky. Each step sounded like a gunshot, especially the third one from the top. But my mom didn't wake up.

I yanked open the refrigerator and looked at the contents. I felt hungry enough to eat everything in the fridge. I was skinny. Skinnier than any kid in my grade. The other kids teased me that I was a skeleton. When I took my shirt off in the gym locker room, you could count my ribs.

I made myself a sandwich. With roast beef from the

good deli that my mom bought specifically for my dad. Muenster cheese. Lots of mayonnaise and Dijon mustard. My mouth watered looking at it.

But just as I sat down at the kitchen table, I heard the crash from upstairs.

It had come from my mother's room. I took a quick bite of my sandwich, then pushed my chair back and stood up again. What was she *doing* up there?

I took the stairs more briskly on the way up. My parents' bedroom was at the end of the hallway. I listened for another sound. But it was quiet.

I carefully walked to the end of the hallway. Dimly, it occurred to me that maybe my mom had the key to the gun case. Maybe she thought *I* was the one driving my father away and she had the same plan I did. Pretend she heard an intruder, then blow me away.

Would she really do something like that?

When I got to her bedroom, I pressed my ear against the door. No sound. I rapped my fist against it.

"Mom?"

Again, no answer.

My stomach was doing flip-flops. Maybe she was just asleep. Except what was that loud crash?

I reached out and slowly turned the doorknob. The first thing I saw was the body sprawled out on the floor. My mom, right next to the bed. Passed out on the carpet, a trail of drool leaking from her lips.

I stared at her a moment. Why was she asleep on the carpet?

And then I saw the pill bottles on the nightstand. Four of them.

I stepped over my mother's body, and I took a closer

look at the bottles. They were all empty. I picked up the first bottle. *Take one pill for difficulty sleeping.*

I sank onto the bed as I realized what she had done. She took all the pills in the house. And now she was passed out on the floor, probably needing her stomach pumped like I heard Dan Chadwick did at the New Year's Eve party I didn't get invited to.

And if that didn't happen, she would die.

I put the pill bottle back on her nightstand. I crept over her body and left the room, closing the door behind me. Then I went downstairs and finished my sandwich.

CHAPTER 31

CLAIRE

The cabin looks empty.

It's dead silent, first of all. There's a beat-up sofa in the middle of what appears to be the living room, with rips in it and stuffing coming out of one of the pillows. There's a small fireplace that's covered in a layer of soot, a half-size bookcase with a few hardcovers and paperbacks inside, and a kitchen alcove with a sink and a gray-tinged, rusty refrigerator.

Oh my God. A sink!

All three of us run for the sink. Jack gets there first and hits one of the faucets. I almost cry with happiness when water comes out of the tap. Water! Clean water that's slightly tinged with brown but at least doesn't have flecks of mud in it. And we don't have to ration it. We can drink as much as we want!

There are glasses in the cabinet above the sink, and Jack passes them around. The glasses look grimy and smudged, but it doesn't matter. We each fill up our glasses and drink until we have finished the contents, then we go back for seconds. The water has a metallic aftertaste, but I could not care less. It tastes like fine wine after what we've been drinking the last two days.

"Hey," Noah says after we have all downed two brimming glasses of water, "look at this."

He's pointing at the rickety, circular kitchen table. There's a plastic chair set up in front of the table. But the really strange thing is there's a plate on the table. With a sandwich on it. Two bites have been taken out of the sandwich. And there's also a half-full glass of water.

"So there *is* somebody here!" I say, probably too loud.

Jack narrows his eyes at the food on the table. He lifts his rifle and points in the direction of what seems to be the bedroom. The door is closed tightly.

"Knock on the door," Noah says. "If there's somebody in there, we'll just explain our situation. Hopefully, they'll understand."

Jack quietly and slowly makes his way over to the bedroom door. Noah steps in front of me and whispers, "Get ready to duck down."

Jack hesitates at the door. He lifts his hand, then knocks gently. No answer.

"Hello?" he calls.

No response.

"We're, uh…" He clears his throat. "We've been lost in the woods and…"

Still no response.

Jack glances back at us. "I'm going to open the door."

Noah nods. I clutch Noah's arm so tightly I must be hurting him, but he doesn't say anything.

Just like at the front door, Jack reaches for the knob

and it turns easily. He clutches his rifle in both hands and kicks the door open gently with his foot. Nobody comes out shooting, so I count that as a win. I hold my breath as he kicks the door the rest of the way open and steps into the bedroom.

"Empty!" he calls.

What the…?

Jack looks in the bathroom too, and that's also empty. My elation at not having to crouch down in a bush anymore to pee is tempered by my uneasiness about this entire situation. Even though we haven't found anyone in this cabin, somebody is living here. I mean, there's a half-eaten sandwich on the table. Nobody goes home from their vacation cabin and leaves half-eaten food on the table. Well, most people wouldn't.

I go over to the bedroom and look inside. There's a small twin mattress in the center of the room on a rusted metal bed frame. Some covers are lying in a pile in the center of the bed. I'm not saying whoever lives here was obligated to make their bed, but it seems like a place where somebody has slept recently. Very recently.

"There's got to be somebody living here," I say.

Jack shrugs. "I don't know what to tell you. There's nobody here. And I don't see a car. How would somebody get here without a car?"

"Has anyone seen a phone?" Noah asks.

That's a great question. I take my cell phone out of my purse, hoping the battery has suddenly come back to life. No such luck. Noah is in the same boat. Jack was smart enough to turn off his phone early on, but when he turns it on now, he still has no reception.

But this place may have a landline. We start to search.

As I walk around the dilapidated cabin, I still can't shake the feeling that someone was living here very, very recently. That sandwich. Somebody was eating that sandwich. It doesn't look like it's been sitting on the table for months. It looks fresh.

I check out the contents of the refrigerator. It's not packed to the brim, but it's well stocked. There's bread and lunch meat. And a container of milk. I pull out the carton of milk and look at the expiration date. It's three days from today.

"A phone jack!" Noah calls out.

I run over to where he's pointing. There's a jack in the wall of the cabin for a phone to be plugged in. Except there's nothing plugged into it. No phone.

"Well, that's not helpful," Jack grumbles.

Why wouldn't the person living here have a phone? Or are they some sort of recluse? The cabin doesn't seem to have electricity either. Jack says the refrigerator is running on gas power, so that's fine. I don't need electricity. I'm just happy about the running water and food.

Since the search for a phone has not come up with anything, we decide to eat some lunch and figure out our next move. Noah makes us all sandwiches, and it takes all my willpower not to scarf mine down in three bites.

"I think we should stay put," Noah says. "We've got food and running water. Claire's sister probably knows something is wrong by now because we haven't checked on the kids. I'm sure somebody has started searching for us."

"I agree," Jack says.

"Yes." I agree with them in theory. I don't want to leave this cabin and go back out there. But at the same time, something about this place is making me very uncomfortable. "But what if the person living here comes back?"

"That would be good," Jack says. "They probably have a car and might be able to drive us to the inn."

"Yeah." I look around the cabin, which is reeking with the presence of another person who was here very recently. "But what happened to the person who is living here? I mean, who leaves their home with a half-eaten sandwich on the table?"

Jack raises his hand. "I've done that."

"You have?"

He shrugged. "Sure. You make yourself a sandwich. Then you forget about it when you get a phone call. And then you leave the house with the sandwich still on the table."

I don't entirely buy it. I look over at Noah, who has the same uneasy expression on his face that I do. Someone is living here. Someone left this house in a great hurry. And I would like to know what happened to them.

CHAPTER 32

CLAIRE

Even though I probably shouldn't, I investigate the bedroom. Meaning I go through the drawers, looking for a clue as to who lives here.

It doesn't take long to verify that the occupant of this cabin is a man. There's absolutely nothing feminine about this rustic cabin in the middle of nowhere. The bedroom has one unfinished wooden dresser, and I pull the top drawer open. The first thing I see is a heavy hardcover copy of the Bible. Apparently, a religious person lives here.

I shove the Bible to the side and pull out a pair of blue jeans. I hold them up against my chest. It looks like the owner of these pants is about a foot taller than I am and quite a bit heavier. I don't feel like running into this person. Not when I'm intruding in his house.

He has a little night table by the bed. There's a glass of water on the table with about an inch of water inside. I imagine the big, tall man lying in his bed and taking a drink of water before going to sleep. Maybe reading a little bit of the Bible first.

I haven't read the Bible in years. My family always made me go to church when I was a kid, but I dropped the habit as an adult. Noah is also a nonpracticing Christian and never seemed terribly interested in organized religion. But there's something about having the Bible in the room with me that's comforting.

I pick up the hardcover book. It feels lighter than I would have expected. I wonder if there's an inscription inside that will tell me the name of the owner. I turn to the first page, and my mouth falls open.

The Bible has been hollowed out. There's an imprint inside in the shape of a small gun. Except it's empty.

I drop the copy of the Bible back onto the dresser, my hands shaking. What's going on here? Where is the gun that used to be kept in this Bible?

Noah comes running in at the sound of the book falling onto the floor. His eyes are wide and his hair looks even more disheveled than usual. "What happened? I heard a noise."

I back away from the dresser, suddenly embarrassed for having been snooping. Noah is looking at me with his head cocked to the side, and I know I should tell him about the Bible. But somehow, I don't.

"I'm fine," I say.

He stifles a yawn. "I started dozing off on the sofa. It's not very comfortable, but I'm so damn tired."

I slept horribly last night, but I've never been so awake in my life. "Maybe you should try out the bed."

"Yeah." Noah glances at the unmade bed. "I feel bad about stealing the guy's bed, but… Well, I can change the sheets before we leave."

I nod. "I…I think I'm going to go outside and get some fresh air."

He frowns. "Do you want me to go with you?"

I shake my head. "No, you get some rest. I just need to clear my head."

Noah is quiet for a moment, and I wonder if he's going to insist on going with me. Part of me hopes he does. Through this entire thing, he's been so reassuring. He keeps telling me he's going to get us home. He doesn't seem scared at all.

But finally, he says, "Okay. But if you change your mind, wake me up."

"I will." I glance past his shoulder into the living room. "Where did Jack go?"

"Off to get some firewood for tonight." He cocks his head to the side. "Why? Do you need him?"

Am I imagining it, or is there a slight edge to his voice? "No, just wondering."

When I get outside, the sun is still up, which means it's hot. The mud on my clothing has dried, and my shorts and shirt feel stiff and uncomfortable. Tonight, I'm going to wash out all my clothes in the sink and hang them up to dry overnight. It would be nice to have another outfit ready in case we need to make a quick getaway, but I desperately want clean clothing. It's worth the risk.

I lean against the side of the cabin, but something scrapes against my back. I turn around to look at the wood of the outer wall. There are five claw marks gouging the desiccated wood. The claw marks are deep enough that I can stick half my index finger inside.

They look just like the ones on the trees in the forest.

I turn around and stare off into the woods surrounding

the cabin. It looks so dark and foreboding. I listen for a minute and hear nothing. I can't believe we were lost out there for two days. But inside the cabin, we'll be safe. Safe from whatever creature was scraping against the wall.

I wonder about the man who lives here. I wonder if he built it himself. The furniture looks homemade. I imagine him being a big, burly guy with a full beard. The sort of guy who keeps a gun in a hollowed-out Bible.

But the real question is: *Where is he?*

Does his absence have anything to do with the claw marks? Are we really safe inside the cabin?

And where is his gun?

Far in the distance, I hear a sound. Like a howl. It's not close, but it's not that far either. I take a step back and hit the wall. I squint at the branches of the tree across from me.

Did those branches just move? Is there someone out there?

"Claire?"

I nearly jump out of my skin. I clutch my chest, trying to catch my breath. It's only Jack. He's standing a few yards away from me, the rifle in his hand. Now that he has it back, he's not going to let it go again. He'll probably sleep on top of it.

"Hey," I say.

As he gets closer, I noticed how pale his face looks. He washed the blood off his hands at the stream, but there's still blood all over his jeans, staining the fabric almost brown. He puts one hand against the wall of the cabin for support. "I need to show you something, Claire."

"What?"

He just shakes his head. "Come with me."

I hesitate. I remember what Noah said yesterday about

how Warner saw Jack and Michelle disappear together into the woods. Of course, it's still daytime, but I have a bad feeling about it. And then there was that howling sound in the distance. Maybe it's not safe. "Should Noah come too?"

"No." He grabs my arm firmly. "Come on. You have to see this."

I feel uneasy, but on the other hand, I don't think Jack means me any harm. And I have to admit, I'm curious what it is he wants to show me so badly.

I follow him, but my misgivings multiply as we get to the edge of the woods to a small, dark path. A few minutes ago, I was swearing to myself I would never go in there again. I haven't changed my mind. The whole time we were in the woods, I had this horrible sense something was hunting us. And that feeling hasn't entirely gone away.

"Jack…"

"Please, Claire." He turns his brown, bloodshot eyes on me. "You need to see this."

Without waiting for my answer, he takes my arm again and drags me along beside him. I'm about to protest, but then he stretches out his arm and shows me something that makes my heart stop in my chest.

CHAPTER 33

CLAIRE

It's a truck. A big green pickup truck, badly rusted in the back, with a big dent in the left fender.

"I knew there had to be a vehicle around here somewhere." He nods in the direction of the truck. "It didn't take me long to find it."

"Why is it parked out here?"

"Come on." Jack takes my arm again. "I'll show you."

I don't know if I want to know anymore, but I dutifully follow Jack to the truck. Maybe this is a way out of here. If we've got a vehicle, we can make it to the main road, hopefully.

As we get closer to the truck, it becomes obvious it's about as beat up as everything else in the cabin. Clearly, the big guy with the Bible gun is the owner. But why did he abandon the truck in the middle of the forest?

"Look at the driver's window," Jack says.

I creep closer, holding on to the side of the truck so I don't lose my balance. Before I even get to the window, I realize the truck isn't empty. There's a man in the driver's seat. A big man with a thick, matted beard and a tangle of graying hair. I take another step closer and I see the vacant look in the large man's dark eyes.

And I scream.

"Shh!" Jack hisses at me. "Keep it down!"

"But…" I lift my eyes again and see the blood all over his chest. Oh God. "He's dead!"

"Right." Jack heaves a sigh. "I found him like this. I think he's got a stab wound in his chest."

Before this week, I'd never been anywhere near a dead person before, and now this is the second one after Lindsay. A wave of nausea comes over me, and this time I've got food in my belly. I have to fight to keep it down.

"Claire," he says, "are you okay?"

"No!" Tears spring to my eyes. How did this become my life? A week ago, I was enjoying a nice evening with my family in my comfortable home. Now I'm out in the middle of nowhere, staring at a dead body. I'm never going to make it back home—I know it. "No, I'm *not* okay! How did…"

Jack's expression is grim. "The blood on his chest is dry," he says. "This didn't just happen."

I frown at him. "Wait, were you inside the truck?"

"I had to go inside. I wanted to see if the keys were in there."

"And?"

He shakes his head. "Couldn't find them anywhere. Even looked in the guy's pockets."

I'm impressed he had the nerve. You couldn't get me in a truck with a dead guy if you paid me a million bucks.

"But it hasn't been that long since he was killed." He

glances back in the direction of the cabin. "That sandwich on the table wasn't rotting or anything."

The wheels are turning in my head. The man has a stab wound in his chest. That means the animal that made the claw marks didn't kill him. Whoever killed him had opposable thumbs capable of holding a knife.

He was killed by a human being.

"Do you think..." I take a deep breath, barely even able to get out the words. "Do you think whoever killed him will be back?"

"Well," Jack says thoughtfully, "it depends why they killed him, doesn't it?"

I take a step away from the truck. "We've got to tell Noah about this."

"No!" Jack's tone is sharp. "I don't think we should tell Noah what we know."

"Why on earth not?"

He shuffles between his feet, looking down into the dirt. "It's all kind of a coincidence, don't you think?"

"Coincidence?"

"Your minivan," he says. "That van is practically new. Why would it just suddenly break down?"

I blink at him. "The battery died."

"I don't know a lot about cars, but I know a *little* something." He lifts his eyes to look straight into mine. "The battery in your car looked older than all the other stuff under the hood."

I snort. "That's ridiculous."

"Is it?" A muscle twitches under his eye. "I told you how my compass was giving me wrong directions. I thought it was Warner throwing it off, but I checked the compass again after he disappeared. It was still wrong."

"So?"

"So don't you see?" He lowers his voice. "It had to have been Noah."

"What are you saying?" I blurt out. "You're saying Noah engineered this entire thing? That's the most ridiculous thing I've ever heard."

"That first night, when we were about to go to sleep, we all drank some water," Jack says. "Except Noah was a 'gentleman' and he passed most of it to you, right?"

I do remember how touched I was when he barely drank any water, even though I assumed he was as thirsty as I was. I didn't realize Jack had noticed. "Right."

He chews on his lip. "I thought at the time the water had a strange, chalky taste. And now I'm sure of it. Someone put something in that water."

It did have a strange taste. But still. "That couldn't be true."

"Really? How else did we all sleep so soundly through the night?"

That's a good point. I was surprised at how deeply I slept that night considering I was lying in a bed of leaves. But *Jack* was the one who went off with Michelle that night, not Noah.

Of course, it was Noah who told me that.

"Maybe it's all a game he's playing," Jack says. "He's torturing us as he gets rid of us one by one."

I stare at Jack. I don't care what he says, Noah would never do something like that. This man is my husband. "That's ridiculous. Why would he do something like that?"

Jack lowers his voice. "Because of *us*. Because he knows what's been going on between the two of us."

"He doesn't know."

"I think he does."

I start to protest, but then I remember Lindsay said the same thing. She was certain he knew Jack and I were having an affair. "Even so, he wouldn't do *this*. He just wouldn't!"

"I've known Noah longer than you have, Claire." He folds his arms across his chest. "And I think he absolutely would do something like this under the right circumstances."

"Bullshit."

Jack looks at me for a moment, as if debating something in his head. "Our freshman year of college, Noah's father died. They were really close, and he was a mess."

"I know."

"You know the story," he says, "but you don't know what happened. He was walking around like a zombie for months. Anytime I asked him a question, he would bite my head off. I borrowed some water he was keeping in our mini fridge, and he walked up to me and punched me in the mouth."

I gnaw on my thumbnail. "He punched you?"

"I'm telling you, he was a mess." Jack shakes his head. "And that's how he was acting at the beginning of this trip. Claire, I don't know what he's capable of right now. I'd like to think he couldn't do something like this, but I know I didn't do it, and I know it wasn't you, so…"

"This is the most ridiculous thing I've ever heard in my life." That sick feeling is almost overwhelming. I need to sit down. "Jack, Noah is not a murderer. I know that for sure… I just…I can't have this conversation with you anymore. I…I have to go."

I turn on my heels and run back in the direction of the cabin before Jack can say another word. It turns out that I might've been right about us being hunted. But it wasn't an animal hunting us.

CHAPTER 34

CLAIRE

Jack is extremely subdued during dinner. And so am I.

I make us some sandwiches again. There's a good amount of food in the refrigerator, and the cupboards are packed with canned goods. It will more than get us through the week if it takes that long for somebody to find us. We can survive out here a month or longer if we have to. Hell, we could probably get through a year if we don't mind eating lots of canned beans. And we have unlimited water.

That said, I want to get out of here as soon as possible. I'm dreading even spending the night here.

"We don't want to finish all the fresh food," Noah comments as he chews on his sandwich. "I mean, we want to leave something for when the guy who lives here comes back, right?"

Jack and I exchange looks. *See? If he killed that guy out in the pickup truck, he wouldn't say something like that.*

Or would he?

"So I thought me and Claire could sleep in the bedroom tonight," Noah says. "Do you mind sleeping on the couch, Jack?"

"Yeah, fine," he mumbles.

"Are you sure you're okay with it? I just figured the bed is bigger, so…"

"I said it's fine!" Jack snaps. When Noah goes silent, he stands up from his seat fast enough that the chair nearly falls over. "I'm going out for a walk."

"Now?" I say. "But it's dark out!"

"It's perfectly safe out there," Jack says. I don't fail to notice his emphasis on the words "out there."

He grabs his sweatshirt and his rifle, then leaves the house without another word. I hear the echo of the door slamming behind him.

Noah raises his eyebrows at me. "What's with him?"

"He just…" I hesitate. Even though I don't believe a word of what Jack said about Noah, I still don't want to tell him what I know about the dead guy in the pickup truck. "I think he's worried nobody is looking for us."

"I'm sure somebody is looking for us," Noah says confidently. "I bet tomorrow, we'll be on our way home."

"Yeah." I swallow a big lump in my throat. If only that were true. "I miss the kids."

"Me too." Noah fishes around in his pocket and pulls out his wallet. "The last couple of days, whenever I start getting depressed, I look at this picture."

He slides the photo over to me. It's been creased, having been in his wallet for a long time, but the image is still crisp and clear. It's a picture of me with Emma and Aidan at Emma's birthday last year. She was missing both her front teeth, and Aidan is giving her bunny ears.

They're both beaming with happiness. Looking at the photo makes me want to burst into tears.

"I can't believe you carry around this picture all the time," I manage. It doesn't escape me that there are tons of pictures of the kids without me. He chose to carry one that had me in it.

"Yeah," he says. "It's my favorite."

How could Jack have said Noah is responsible for all the bad things that have happened? He couldn't possibly be. All he wants is to get home to his family. Just like I do.

"Anyway." Noah tugs on his shirt collar. "I'm going to try to clean my clothes tonight. I can't stay in these muddy things another day."

"I know," I say. There's also a shower I would love to get into, but I couldn't seem to get the water to heat up. A cold shower isn't terribly appealing. "I'm going to wash mine, so I can do yours too."

"You don't have to do that."

"I don't mind."

He smiles crookedly. "Okay then."

We both head to the bedroom. As soon as the door is closed, I kick off my muddy sneakers, then peel off my sweaty, dirty socks. It feels so good to wiggle my toes and feel the fresh air. Then I peel off my dirty shorts and shirt. I can't wait to get them clean.

I look up and see that Noah has done the same. He's down to just his boxer shorts.

It's funny. Every single night for over a decade, we have undressed and gotten into bed together. But this feels different. When I look over at Noah's bare chest, I feel something for him that I haven't felt in a long time. Somehow I'd forgotten how good he looked without a shirt on.

And when I meet his eyes, I realize he's looking at me the same way.

"Hey," he says.

"Hey," I say back.

He grins shyly at me. "Have I ever told you how sexy you look in a bra and panties?"

I smile back. "Not lately."

"Well…" He comes around the bed to get closer to me. "That is a huge oversight on my part, and I have to apologize."

"You're forgiven."

He's standing less than a foot away from me. "Am I?"

"Absolutely."

He slowly lowers his lips onto mine, and my whole body tingles the way it did when he first kissed me all those years ago. A second later, he's tugging me into the bed. This trip has been one of the worst experiences of my life, but I think it may have saved my marriage.

As long as we make it home alive.

CHAPTER 35

ANONYMOUS

After my first set of exams in college was over, I drove home.

It was a three-hour drive, but it was worth it. College wasn't like home. Even though my roommate and I got along, I needed time away. I wanted to be back in my own bedroom—not in that cramped dorm room on a stiff twin bed. Moreover, I wanted to see my dad.

After my mother killed herself, my father finally cut back on his time on the road. He was shaken by the whole thing. He wasn't the same guy he used to be. He blamed himself, and the guilt kept him home. It wasn't how I wanted it to happen, but it happened.

He helped me lug my boxes from home to my dorm room, although I did a lot of lifting thanks to his bad back. And that's the last time I saw him. We talked on the phone once a week, but I worried. He looked old when he said goodbye to me at the entrance to my dorm. He wasn't going to be around forever. He didn't eat right and barely exercised. For all I knew, he could have a heart attack before I even finished college.

So that's why I drove out. I asked beforehand to make sure he wasn't going to be on a business trip, but I didn't mention I was coming. I figured we could watch a movie together on TV. Maybe share a couple of beers. Yeah, I wasn't twenty-one yet, but he wasn't bothered by things like that.

By the time I got to the house, it was dark. I hit traffic, and then, when it started to get late, I stopped for fast food. A quarter pounder with cheese. French fries. A chocolate milkshake. My mom never let me have fast food, so I was having too much of it. I was still skinny as a rail though.

I parked on the street since my father's car was in the driveway and I didn't want to block him. The house was dark too. Apparently, he wasn't home, even though his car was there.

It didn't matter. As long as he wasn't away on a business trip, he would be back. He probably went out for a beer with his buddies from work and planned to bum a ride home. It would be good to have the house to myself for a couple of hours.

I let myself into the house and went straight upstairs to my bedroom on the second floor. It was a long drive, and I was tired. I flicked on the lights and dumped my duffel bag with clothing for the weekend on my bed. Then I flopped down on the mattress and shut my eyes.

I must have drifted off to sleep, because the next thing I knew, I could hear the lock turning in the front door. I yawned and sat up in bed, rubbing my eyes. My father was finally home—I could hear his voice.

And another familiar voice.

My heart was pounding. I stood up from the bed and walked over to the door, which was slightly ajar. I peeked outside my bedroom, at the staircase leading to the front door.

My father's voice: "Are you sure you don't want to spend the night?"

"No. I really shouldn't. I have to be up early tomorrow morning."

"Maybe you should just move in here then."

"God, can you imagine what people would say?"

"She's been dead for almost two years, Jeannette. It's been long enough."

"I don't know."

"Fine. Go home. Just let me say goodbye first."

I took a step back as I watched my father kiss my mother's sister.

It was exactly what my mom had accused him of that night she killed herself. She said he was fooling around with her sister. She screamed at him that all his business trips were just excuses to cheat. At the time, I thought she was imagining things. My dad would never do anything like that.

I was wrong.

He was kissing Aunt Jeannette deep enough that he could probably taste her breakfast. He had no idea I was watching.

He tortured my mother. She already had a tenuous grip on reality, and he made it worse. She was always paranoid about losing him, and now I could see why. And he didn't care that she took it out on me. He just let it all happen. His secret life was too important to him.

He said good night to Jeannette and she took off in her white Toyota. I never said a word. I couldn't have, even if I wanted to. I felt too sick to talk.

I stood on the second floor as my dad went into the kitchen. I could hear him pouring himself a drink. He turned on the news and watched for a while. I was dimly aware of the newscasters talking. A child disappeared from a playground downtown. The town elections would be held this week. The forecast was calling for rain tomorrow.

It was nearly an hour later when he finally started up the steps to the second floor. I hadn't budged in all that time. It was only when he got to the top that he saw me standing there.

"Jesus Christ!" He clutched his chest. "I didn't see you there. What the hell are you doing here?"

"You were kissing Aunt Jeannette," I said.

His eyes widened. "You saw that?"

I nodded.

He rubbed at the back of his neck. "Look, sport…"

"Don't call me that."

"Look, I'm sorry." He frowned. "It's complicated. I wish you could understand."

"Complicated?" I repeated. "What's so complicated? I needed you when I was a kid, and you were off messing around with other women. My mother's sister, for chrissake. No wonder she went and lost her mind."

"Oh, you think it was all my fault?" He lifted his eyebrows. "You better own up to your own role. Half the arguments we had were because of you. And your behavior. You think it was easy having a kid like you? Always getting into fights. We had to move after you gouged the eye out of that McCormick kid."

I swallowed, remembering the day Bryan McCormick teased me about my shaved head and my "cooties." I had been so angry—I wanted to hurt him. Badly. "That was an accident."

"Bullshit." He sneered at me. "That poor kid lost his eye because of you. That was no accident."

I bit the inside of my cheek until I tasted blood. It reminded me of the blood that had poured down Bryan's left cheek as he screamed. "He deserved it."

"They always did, didn't they?" he snorted. "I suppose Snowball also deserved what you did to her."

There was a bitter taste in my mouth as I remembered my mother's treasured white cat. The one she loved more than me. I will never forget the look on my mom's face when she discovered what I had done to that cat. All the color had drained from her cheeks, and she clasped a hand over her mouth as her legs gave way beneath her. I hadn't been able to suppress a smile, even when she slapped me hard enough to leave a mark.

Now Snowball was buried in the backyard. My mother was buried in the local cemetery. And Bryan McCormick's eye was long gone.

"Your mother and I had no idea what to do with you," he grunted. "We were scared stiff. Why do you think I locked up my rifle and never let you near it anymore? I thought you'd kill us all while we were sleeping."

"I wouldn't do that."

"Wouldn't you?" His jaw tightened. "Your mother died with you right here in the house, in the very next bedroom. You think I don't know you had something to do with it?"

My face burned. He had come just a little too close to hitting the nail on the head. "Take that back."

"I won't take it back. It's the truth."

I imagined him calling the police. Telling them what he knew. I imagined handcuffs being locked around my wrists.

I gritted my teeth. "Take. It. Back."

He folded his arms across his chest. "I think you ought to leave. I won't call the cops on you, but I want you out of here. For good. I don't want to see you again."

The rage I felt in my body was stronger than anything I had ever felt before. Worse than when I took out Bryan McCormick's eye. I felt like I had no control over my own fists. I reached out and shoved my dad as hard as I could.

Under other circumstances, he would've fallen and maybe bruised a hip. But my father was standing at the edge of the staircase. My shove threw him off balance. His arms flailed for a moment, then down he went.

When he hit the bottom of the staircase, I heard a sickening thump.

I raced down the flight of stairs. My father was lying at the bottom, face down, his head at an odd angle. I watched as a puddle of blood slowly grew beneath him. I stood there for a moment, staring at his body.

My thoughts were racing. If I called the police, what were the chances they would believe it was an accident? Especially when my mother died here only two years earlier.

On the other hand, nobody knew I was here. My car had only been parked outside for a couple of hours, and it was dark out. If I drove away, would anyone question my story? After all, old people fall down the stairs sometimes. Accidents happen.

I took one last look at my father. I had been so angry at him a minute ago, but now I was numb. Yes, he had done something awful. But he paid the price.

I left on the light as I slipped out the front door and locked it behind me.

CHAPTER 36

CLAIRE

It hasn't been this good in a long time. Not since we've been married. Not with Jack. Maybe not *ever*. Something about almost dying results in really fantastic sex.

After it's over, we lie next to each other in bed, my sweaty body draped over his. I feel his hand brush a strand of hair from my face.

"I love you so much, Claire," he says.

"I love you too." A week ago, I thought there was no chance I would've ever said those words to him again. But now I mean it. I love him. "So much."

He squeezes me tighter. "I know things have been rough between us lately, and I'm sorry."

"It wasn't entirely your fault."

"Regardless." He squeezes me again and plants a kiss on my head. "I want to get back to the way we were."

"Me too."

This is what I've been wanting to hear from him.

We've been staying together for the kids, but I hated that. I wanted to be happy with him again.

Except it can't go back to the way it was. Not really. I did something terrible to him. I cheated on him with his best friend. How can we move forward with that skeleton in the closet? The guilt will eat me alive.

But if I tell him, he may never forgive me.

I don't know what to do. But I feel like we can't move forward with a lie between us.

"Noah…" I take a deep breath, trying to steady my voice. "There's something I need to tell you."

"Oh?" His eyebrows bunch together. "What is it?"

"It's…something pretty bad."

"Claire, you're freaking me out." He pulls away to look at me. "What is it?"

It occurs to me that maybe I should have waited until we got home to tell him this. But it's too late now.

"The thing is…" I bite down on the inside of my cheek. Hard. "For the last few months, Jack and I have… well, we…"

"Oh." Noah lets out a sigh. "I know."

"What?" I sit up in bed, clutching the blankets to my chest. "You know that Jack and I—"

He raises his hand. "You don't have to say it. Yes, I know."

"But…for how long?"

"For a while. You weren't exactly subtle."

I stare at him, trying to read the expression on his face. Lindsay and Jack both tried to convince me that he knew, but I didn't believe it. They were right.

"Look"—he props himself up into a sitting position on the creaky twin mattress—"what you did…it was bad.

But it was partially my fault. Our marriage was a disaster. The truth is that I also…"

I suck in a breath. "You had an affair?"

"No. *No.* But…" He picks at a loose thread on the pillowcase. "I mean, since we're being honest, there was…a woman. And…nothing happened. Not exactly. But…"

"But?"

He hangs his head. "I kissed her." He quickly adds, "And that's it. Nothing more happened. I stopped it. I just…" He sighs. "I was mad at you. I wanted to get back at you. But all I could think of when it was happening was that she wasn't you. And…I wanted to do whatever it took to get you back. *Anything.*"

My heart is thudding in my chest. I can't believe Noah kissed another woman. Part of me hates him for it. But I did something so much worse, it's almost a relief to know he had a moment of weakness too.

"I had been hoping this trip would be a good chance for us to reconnect." He winces. "But then when you told me you got separate rooms for us, I thought, well, it's over."

I drop my eyes. "I thought it was over too."

He reaches out and takes my hand in his. "I know this is stupid, but even when we were back in college, I used to imagine us growing old together. I knew you were the one. I was so *sure.* When I thought it was over, I just… It was like my future was gone."

I squeeze his hand. "I know."

I fall back into his arms. I feel drained with the guilt of the last several months finally out of my system. Noah knows what happened, and he forgives me. Soon we'll go back home together and restart our lives. We won't fight all the time like we used to. We'll grow old together, just like we planned to.

Everything is going to be okay.

CHAPTER 37

CLAIRE

Noah drifts off to sleep, but I'm having more trouble falling asleep. It seems like after how well I slept for two nights when I was on the ground, I would go to sleep instantly in an actual bed. But somehow, it doesn't work that way.

After an hour of trying, I extract myself from Noah's embrace and slip out of bed. We never ended up cleaning our clothing, so I may as well do that now.

I gather up my shirt, shorts, and socks from the ground, then go to pick up Noah's blue jeans. But as I'm pulling them from the floor, something falls out of the pocket. A glimmer of red.

I bend down to see what the object is. My fingers close around something cold and metallic.

It's a Swiss Army knife.

Why does Noah have a Swiss Army knife? He never mentioned he was carrying a knife. It seems like the sort of thing you might say at some point. Like, *Hey, I'm not just happy to see you, I've got a knife in my pocket.*

I can't help but think about the stab wound in the chest of that man in the pickup truck.

But Noah couldn't have done that. How could he? He was with us the whole time.

Unless he snuck off while we were sleeping…

No. He couldn't have. It's too far.

Although it wasn't as far to the cabin from our campsite as I would've thought. Once we started traveling north, we hit the cabin pretty quickly. If he knew where he was going and walked briskly, he could have easily made it to the cabin, killed that guy, and returned to our campsite.

But *why*?

It couldn't be because of me and Jack. I told him about it, and he wasn't that angry. I mean, he wasn't *thrilled*. But he didn't seem like he was in a jealous rage.

I look over at Noah asleep on the bed. His lips are slightly parted and he's snoring softly. I've known him for nearly half my life. I've been married to him for a decade. He wouldn't do something like that. I know it.

I put down the clothing on the foot of the bed. I pick up the Swiss Army knife and stare down at it in my palm. I tug at the blade until it pops open. I run my finger along the metal, checking for traces of blood.

It's clean.

I let out a sigh. I'm letting my imagination run wild. Noah is my husband. I *know* him. He would never do the things Jack accused him of.

But before I leave the room with our pile of clothing, I slip the Swiss Army knife into one of the dresser drawers and I cover it with clothing.

As I close the door to the bedroom behind me, the front door to the cabin swings open. I clutch the bundle of clothing to my chest as Jack stomps into the room. He raises his eyes to look at me in my bra and panties, and I do my best to conceal myself.

"It's nothing I haven't seen before," he says.

My face burns. "Still."

He shrugs. "Whatever."

"Do you..." I cough. "Would you like me to clean your clothing too?"

"Nah, that's okay." Jack plops down onto the sofa. "I want to be able to make a quick getaway if I need to."

I want to tell him he's being silly, but it's hard to say that with any conviction when there's a dead man within throwing distance of the cabin.

"Listen, Claire." Jack looks up at me with those brown puppy-dog eyes that I thought I had fallen in love with. "If anything happens, scream as loud as you can. I'll come help you."

"Nothing is going to happen," I mumble.

Jack rests the rifle down beside him on the sofa. "Damn straight."

CHAPTER 38

CLAIRE

Somehow it's even more strange to wake up in the cabin. Because in the woods, we were a long way from home. But here, I'm in a bedroom. I'm lying next to Noah. I'm even on the same side of the bed that I sleep on at home. But I'm not home. I'm in a stranger's home. A dead stranger's home.

Also, Noah's arms are wrapped around my body, his left arm protectively resting over me. We haven't slept that way in a very long time. Like spoons.

Our clothing is hanging on the dresser. My shorts and T-shirt look dry by now. I carefully disentangle myself from Noah's arms and walk over to the dresser to check. My shirt feels stiff but dry.

I get dressed and do my best to comb out my hair with my fingers, then gather it back into a ponytail. I put on my clean socks and then my dirty sneakers. The last thing I do is sift through the top drawer for Noah's pocket knife. It's not like I would use it, but it would be comforting to have it.

But when I feel around inside the drawer, the knife is gone.

Noah is still snoring softly in the bed. Did he take the knife back? If so, why? Or did somebody else come into the bedroom and take it while the two of us slept?

I look at the door to the bedroom. Would I have heard it if somebody crept inside during the night?

No, I'm being paranoid. Nobody came into the room while we were sleeping. Noah probably found it and put it somewhere safe. As soon as he wakes up, I'll ask him about it. But I won't wake him now. I'll let him sleep in. I'm jealous—I wish my thoughts weren't racing a mile a minute. I might be able to sleep in.

I bet Jack is awake.

I carefully open the door to the bedroom, trying not to let it creak too loudly. My sneakers thud softly against the ground. As I shut the door behind me, my eyes go straight to the couch where Jack spent the night.

He's gone.

"Jack?" I call out.

Unsurprisingly, there's no reply. If he were in this tiny living space, I would see him.

I walk over to the sofa. His shoes and socks are gone. So is the rifle. Maybe he went to take a walk again.

Except somehow, I don't think so.

I turn back to the bedroom, not bothering to be quiet this time. I shake Noah awake. He yawns, rubbing his eyes with the backs of his hands. "Claire, what's wrong?"

"Jack's gone!" My fingertips are tingling. I might be hyperventilating. "I can't find him!"

"Calm down." He sits up in bed and rubs his eyes again. "He probably went for another walk."

"I don't think he did." I squeeze my hands together. "This is just like what happened with Michelle. And then Warner. We woke up and they were just…gone."

Noah doesn't seem to be taking this seriously enough. He does swing his legs over the edge of the bed, but he makes no move to get up and get dressed. "This is different though. We're in a cabin. It's not like some wild animal came in here and attacked him."

"This is just like what happened the last two nights," I say again.

There were six of us when we started. And one by one, each of us has disappeared. And now there's just me and Noah.

A little voice in my head tells me that I must be next. That I should make a run for it. While I still can. But where could I go? And anyway, if Noah and I are the only ones left, that means that *he* must be responsible for the other people disappearing. And I know that's not the case.

Noah finally drags himself out of bed and puts his clothes on so slowly I want to shake him. He follows me out of the bedroom, but he seems very unimpressed when I point to the sofa.

"I don't know what to say." He scratches at his messy hair. "Do you want to go outside and look for him?"

"Yes," I say.

Maybe Noah is right. Maybe Jack did go out for a walk. Maybe we'll go outside and see him alive and well, and I'll admit I was getting worked up over nothing. I hope so, at least.

Noah goes to the kitchen to pour himself a glass of water, but I'm too antsy. I go to the front door and push it open. And that's when I see it.

Blood. All over the doorstep to the cabin. So much blood.

So much blood.

"Claire?"

I try to answer, but my voice comes out strangled.

There were six of us in the beginning. Now there are only two. And I haven't done this.

"Claire?"

I whirl around to face my husband. He takes a long drink of his glass of water and places it on the kitchen table. He steps toward me, and I take a step back.

"Claire," he says again, "what's wrong?"

"There…" I can barely get the word out. "There's blood…"

"Blood?" His voice sounds flat, disinterested. "What do you mean?"

"It's…it's all over the ground in front of the cabin."

"All over the ground?" His eyes darken. "What are you saying?"

There's something very unfamiliar in Noah's face. Oh God. How did I not see this before? Jack was right. Noah knew about my affair, and he never forgave me for it. I'm such a fool.

He planned this whole thing. This is his revenge. He set us up. He's been killing us one by one.

And now I'm the last one left.

I've got to run. But where? I've got nothing but the clothes on my back. No food, no water. I don't even have my purse with my phone anymore. If I run away from him, what are the chances I'll ever find help in time? If I leave this cabin, I'm dead for sure.

Noah takes another step toward me. "Claire…"

But if I stay, I'm dead for sure.

I jerk my head around. The door is open behind me. It's my only chance.

I take off running as fast as I can. At first, I'm not sure which way to go, but then I remember the truck. It looked like there was a path ahead of the truck that was clear. Maybe it goes somewhere. It's the only chance I've got.

I run as fast as I can. I'm vaguely aware of stepping on a branch and my right ankle twisting slightly, but I ignore the pain. I've got to get out of here.

As I get closer to the truck, I realize another person is sitting inside the cab. It's Jack—sitting there, next to the dead guy. I almost cry with relief. Maybe he's trying to hot-wire it and get it running. Maybe Noah didn't have a chance to get to him after all.

I hold on to the side of the truck, attempting to keep my balance, and I wince at the pain in my right ankle. Jack will know what to do. He's been my rock for the last several months. He's going to get us out of here. Thank God for Jack.

"Jack!" I cry.

I wrench open the passenger-side door to the truck with my right hand. It takes me a split second to realize Jack is not attempting to hot-wire the truck. He's not attempting to do anything. He's just sitting there in the passenger seat, a bullet hole in his forehead.

No way an animal did *that*.

"No." I clasp a hand over my mouth and back away from the truck. "No… No no no no no…"

It's too late.

"Claire, step away from the truck please."

I'm only vaguely aware of the toneless voice giving

me instructions. All I can think is that the man I loved betrayed me. I'm never going to see my children again. I'm going to die out here in the woods.

"Claire."

I turn around slowly, expecting to see Noah with that missing gun pointed at me. Or maybe Jack's rifle. But it's not Noah at all.

It's Warner.

He's got Jack's rifle pointed at me. His blue eyes are dark and foreboding. This is not somebody who you say no to.

"Would you please put your hands in the air, Claire?" Warner says. "Otherwise you'll end up like your friend over there."

My head is spinning. Why is *Warner* here? He disappeared. There was all that blood. We all thought he was dead for sure.

But of course, we never saw his dead body. We just assumed.

"You," I manage. "You did all this."

A chilling smile plays on Warner's lips. "Well, I can't entirely take credit."

That's when it all falls into place. Noah wanted revenge for my betrayal. But he couldn't do it alone. He needed a partner in crime. Somebody to sneak off during the night and kill the man in the cabin while he was pretending to be sound asleep beside me.

But how did Noah even know Warner?

Unless he set it all up at the beginning. He gave poor Lindsay the meet-cute he knew she'd been hoping for, allowing this handsome man to infiltrate our lives. He even knew what zodiac sign Warner needed to be. It was too easy.

"Let's head back to the cabin," Warner says calmly.

He points the rifle at me, and I have every reason to believe he will shoot me if I don't comply. My ankle screams in pain but I push myself to march back to the cabin, where Noah is waiting inside.

I wonder what their plan is. It looks like everyone else was simply murdered, but they want something different for me. Torture. As horrible as it sounds, I can't entirely blame him. I did something terrible to Noah. It made him crack, the way he did when his father died.

God, I wish I still had Noah's Swiss Army knife. If only I had held on to it…

The door to the cabin is still sitting open. Warner marches me inside with my hands still up in the air. The first thing I see when I walk into the living room is Noah. I expected him to have a gun in his hand, pointed at me. But instead, he's sitting on the couch, his head down, his hands raised into the air like mine.

Because somebody else is pointing a gun at his head.

Oh my God.

CHAPTER 39

ANONYMOUS

The first thing Claire Jennings did when I met her was hug me.

"It's so good to finally meet you, Lindsay!" she cried.

I stood there stiffly, accepting her unprompted hug. "It's good to meet you too."

Claire was a hugger. It was one of the things I learned about her during our four years as roommates. She would hug you when she met you. She would hug you after a few days apart. Sometimes she would hug you just because.

She was open and warm and sweet in a way I'd never experienced before. She was my first true friend. She loved me in a way my parents never did. She thought that I was a good person. We laughed together every day. I had never been so happy as I was when I lived with Claire. I would have done anything for my best friend.

I never told her the true story about my childhood. I made up a happier version of the truth. There was no reason for her to think I was lying. She thought I was just like her. Or if she suspected differently, she didn't let on.

During our sophomore year, Claire started dating a boy named Ted. I never liked him very much—I didn't like the way he leered at me or his suggestive comments. My suspicions were later confirmed when she caught him cheating with another girl. Not just another girl but a friend of hers. She was devastated. She spent hours crying, but I did what I could to cheer her up.

I didn't plan what happened to Ted. Not exactly.

When we ran into each other during the summer, he didn't even recognize me as Claire's roommate. He was the counselor at some sort of camp, and he hit on me shamelessly, even though Claire had emailed me a week earlier saying she thought they might be getting back together.

I wasn't surprised Ted was interested in me. I was very attractive. I wasn't on the first day of school, but the freshman fifteen actually did me some favors. I started dressing in more stylish clothing than the tomboy outfits my parents bought me because they always wanted a boy. I also finally managed to grow my hair out. It was amazing having long, silky hair instead of the severely short cut my mother always gave me in the upstairs bathroom. For the first time in my life, I had boobs. Ted couldn't keep his grimy paws off me.

I accepted his invitation to go out on the lake that evening in one of the rowboats he would "borrow" from the camp. It had to be a secret, because he could get in trouble with the camp for taking the boat. Nobody knew we were sneaking off together—I certainly never told Claire.

Ted never returned from the lake that night.

Claire was sad about Ted's untimely death, but she

moved on. She started dating Noah Matchett, the boy living next door to us. You could tell just from talking to him that he was a nice guy. He would treat her right. And sure enough, he married her shortly after we graduated. And he was a very good husband.

I never met anyone like Noah. All the boys (and later men) that I dated were like my father. Too handsome, too charming, and unable to keep it in their pants. But I expected it—I never cried when my boyfriends ultimately did what I knew they would do all along.

My friends were not as smart as I was. I remember the year after I graduated from college, my friend Daphne came to me crying that she had caught her live-in boyfriend in bed with another woman when she came home early from her night shift. She was devastated. She could barely get out of bed for months after. It was some solace when her boyfriend was killed in a hit-and-run not long after.

I found that when you're an attractive woman, it's very easy to get a mechanic to replace your dented front fender without asking too many questions.

There were others. I don't need to get into the details. But trust me, every single one of them deserved it. The same way my parents deserved it.

Claire remained my best friend all those years, and she never knew the truth. If not for me, she might have gotten back together with Ted. She never would have met the love of her life. There were times when I wanted so badly to tell her, but I couldn't be sure she would understand. I didn't want her to look at me the way my parents did.

And then, one day, everything changed.

It started out innocent—I swear. I had borrowed a pair

of earrings from Claire, and I went to her house to return them. I showed up at a time when I thought she would be back from work, but her car wasn't in the driveway. I should've turned away then and gone home. If I had, maybe everything would've turned out different. But I figured I would drop the earrings off while I was there. They were Claire's favorite earrings, after all—she was always very generous with her belongings. It was one of the many things I loved about her.

I rang the doorbell to the Matchetts' beautiful white house and waited. Noah finally showed up at the door, wearing jeans and a T-shirt, a five-o'clock shadow on his chin. He looked mildly embarrassed.

"Claire isn't here," he said.

"Oh, that's okay." I smiled apologetically. "I just wanted to return some earrings I borrowed."

Noah took the baggie with the earrings in it. He looked like he was about to close the door, but then he hesitated. "Claire will be home soon. Do you want to wait?"

"Oh." I hadn't seen Claire in a few weeks, and I had been hoping to have a chance to catch up. "Sure."

The Matchetts' bathroom was like the rest of the house. Clean and homey with powder-blue hand towels. I loved their bathroom. After I washed my hands, I stood there for a moment in the center of the room, breathing in the aroma of their apple-scented hand soap that was running low.

When I finished in the bathroom, Noah was coming out of the basement. "I told Claire I would switch the laundry from the washer to the dryer. She'll kill me if I don't do it."

Claire had been complaining a lot that Noah was reluctant to do chores. She said that everything she asked him to do resulted in an argument. I tried to stay out of it. I figured they would eventually get past their problems. Noah and Claire loved each other. They were nothing like my parents.

"Would you like anything to drink?" Noah asked me.

I settled down on one of the stools by their kitchen counter. "Sure. What do you have?"

He went over to the fridge and scanned the contents. "Uh…do you want Yoo-hoo? Milk? Orange juice?" He looked up and he offered a lopsided smile. "We also have beer."

"Beer?"

He shrugged sheepishly.

"Sure," I said. "Why not?"

He pulled two bottles of Bud Light out of the fridge. He handed one to me and kept the other for himself.

I didn't know what those two beers would lead to. And I didn't know that Claire wasn't going to be home anytime soon. I swear, I didn't come to Claire's house with the intention of kissing her husband. But somehow, in the time we were talking, I noticed he was looking at me *that way*. Many men had looked at me *that way* before, but in all the years I knew him, Noah Matchett had never looked at me like that. Not even once. I had thought he was immune to my charms. But apparently not.

And before I knew it, his lips were on mine.

I enjoyed it. For a split second. I hadn't kissed a man in over a year—at some point, I had gotten sick of the dating scene and given up on it. It felt nice. I won't lie and say he wasn't a very good kisser.

I'm ashamed to admit it was Noah who pulled away first. His face was red and he had a panicked look in his eyes.

"I'm sorry." He got up from his stool so abruptly he nearly tripped on it. "This was a mistake. I can't cheat on Claire."

My cheeks burned with shame. "*You're* the one who kissed *me*."

"I know, I know." He ran a shaking hand through his hair. "I only did it because… Look, it doesn't matter. It was a mistake. You…you better go."

I got out of there as quickly as I could. But before I got home, I sat in my car for an hour, hating myself. I had done something terrible. I betrayed my best friend by kissing her husband. How could I live with myself? I was as bad as my father.

I had to tell Claire the truth.

A week later, Claire and I had lunch together. Over the last several years, she had been looking more and more miserable. Like the life was being sucked out of her. I couldn't remember the last time I saw her without circles under her eyes. She didn't smile and laugh the way she used to.

But this time, she seemed happy. The happiest I had seen her in years. It made me think maybe I shouldn't tell her the truth about Noah. I didn't want to wreck her happiness. And it's not like anything really terrible had happened. It was just a kiss.

"You're in such a good mood," I remarked to her. "Are things…better with Noah?"

"Well…not really." She hesitated before her face broke out in a smile. "But there are other things in life, you know?"

I thought she was talking about her job as a teacher, which I knew she loved. Or her children, who she adored. I still hadn't worked up the nerve to tell her the truth when she got up to go to the bathroom. Claire left her phone behind on the table, and when she was gone, a text message from Jack Alpert popped up on the screen:

> Can't stop thinking about you. Can't wait to see you tomorrow.

Of course, there was only one conclusion I could draw. Claire was cheating on Noah.

Suddenly, it all made sense.

The reason Claire was so happy. The reason Noah felt the need to try to kiss me. She was betraying him. With his best friend. And that was why Noah tried to return the favor with Claire's best friend, except he couldn't go through with it.

I had always thought Claire was the best person I'd ever met. I believed her to be honest and kind and loyal. Now I realized none of that was true. She was betraying the man she had pledged her life to in the worst way imaginable. She was no better than my father, who slept with his wife's own sister. And then Noah tried to use me to get back at her.

It was despicable. They were despicable.

When she arrived back at the table and looked down at her text message, a secret smile touched her lips. I wanted to scratch her eyes out like I did to Bryan McCormick.

I could have confronted her. I could have demanded she break off her affair.

But instead, I decided to do something much worse.

Of course, none of it would have happened if I hadn't met Warner. I met him years earlier, when he gave me some advice online about a poison that would never show up in an autopsy. We got together at my apartment and had a night of spectacular sex together. But I knew he was somebody I didn't want to get involved with, and not just because he was far too handsome and far too charming. He was dangerous. But we still spoke every once in a while, and sometimes we got together for a little fun.

Anyway, I confided in him about everything. We agreed that my former friends deserved to be taught a lesson. Like me, this wasn't his first rodeo. Together, we made a plan. It started out with a phony map and a knife that could carve a tree to look like animal claws.

CHAPTER 40

CLAIRE

indsay," I gasp.

My best friend of over fifteen years raises her blue eyes to look at me. She's got a small pistol in her hand, and she's aiming it at Noah's head. The momentary relief I feel at the realization that she is still alive is overwhelmed by disbelief at what I'm seeing.

"Hello, Claire." She flashes me the smile that made every guy she met fall in love with her. "Welcome back."

My head is filled with too many questions. I don't know which one to ask first. I open my mouth and finally blurt out, "But you're dead!"

Lindsay waves her hand. "Those rumors are highly exaggerated."

"But you ate the deadly nightshade!" I cry.

She clucks her tongue. "I told you those were blueberries, Claire. I know the difference—my mother used to grow them. You should have tried one. They were quite tasty."

"But…but Warner said…" I look over at Warner, still gripping the rifle. I finally get it. "He just told us you were dead. You were fine all along."

"Bingo!" Her smile widens. "It was quite a performance, wasn't it? I think I missed my calling as an actress."

"We watched YouTube videos of people having seizures as research," Warner adds. "And I thought my chest compressions looked very realistic. I didn't hurt you too badly, did I, babe?"

Lindsay shakes her head. "Not at all."

Noah lifts his head just enough that I can see his hazel eyes. He shakes his head ever so slightly.

"You…you killed Jack?" I whisper.

"No." She nods at Warner. "He killed Jack. And the big gentleman who used to own the cabin. But I killed Michelle. And I'm going to kill you."

It feels like somebody knocked all the wind out of me. Noah's face has gone completely white. This can't be happening. Lindsay is my best friend. How could she do this to me? And why?

"Why are you doing this?" I whimper.

Lindsay beams at me. She still looks so pretty, even when she's pointing a gun at my husband. "That's the best part. I'm going to let Noah tell you."

I frown. "Noah?"

Noah drops his face into his hands. "I'm so sorry, Claire. I told you there was a woman that I…"

My mouth falls open. I finally get it. Lindsay, my best friend, was the woman he kissed. I was screwing around with his best friend, so this was the ultimate revenge. But he never went through with it.

"He used me." The smile drops off Lindsay's face as she

hits him in the back of the head with her gun. He flinches but doesn't make a sound. "He tried to use me to get back at you for the disgusting thing you did with Jack." She grimaces. "Both of you are horrible people."

"Lindsay," Noah murmurs, "that's not what happened."

"Shut the fuck up, Noah," she snaps. She turns back to look at me. "You had it all. You had a great life with a perfect husband. If I knew you were going to screw it up, I never would've bothered to get rid of Ted."

"Ted..." It takes me a moment to realize what she's talking about. Ted—my boyfriend during my sophomore year. The one who drowned over the summer. "Oh my God, Lindsay, you didn't..."

Her eyes fill with fire. "He deserved it. He was an awful person, Claire. He would have betrayed you again and again. I had to do it to *save* you."

I cover my mouth, unable to believe what I'm hearing. Lindsay killed Ted all those years ago. Because of *me*.

I had no idea what she was capable of.

But now I know. She's got a gun in her hand and it's clear she intends to use it. She's going to kill us. I'm never going to make it home. I'm never going to see Emma and Aidan again. They're going to grow up without us.

My eyes meet Noah's for a split second. This might be one of the last times I see him. Last night with him... It was wonderful. I made a terrible mistake when I slept with Jack. I should never have done it. I should have tried to work things out with Noah first.

And now I'm paying the ultimate price.

"Lindsay," Noah says quietly, "you're making a big mistake. You don't want to do this. You'll go to jail for the rest of your life."

"No, I don't think she will," Warner speaks up. I had nearly forgotten he was standing behind me until I hear his baritone. "We've got the perfect alibi. I'd really love for you to hear it."

I feel sick. I don't want to hear anything this man has to say, but maybe if he keeps talking, we can figure out a way to get out of this.

"So here's what we'll tell the police." He nods at Noah. "Noah here discovered his wife was cheating on him with his best friend. He flew into a horrible, jealous rage. Then…he killed everyone in the room, including himself. Fortunately, Lindsay and I were out for a walk when it happened, and we came back just in time to see the carnage."

Noah's face blanches. "You're not really…"

Lindsay cocks her head to the side. "Sad, isn't it? Your children will grow up without parents and also thinking their father was a murderer." She shrugs. "But what's the difference? It's not like either of you cared about the fact that you were ripping apart your family. Emma begged you to stay home, but you came here anyway."

I flinch at the memory of Emma's small face looking up at me, pleading with me not to go on this trip. If only I had listened to her. I could be with my children right now.

Noah's right hand balls into a fist. He looks like he wants to hit one or both of them. At this point, maybe he should. They're going to kill us anyway. We may as well go out swinging.

"There's only one little detail," Lindsay says.

She raises the gun and points it directly at Noah's skull. I squeeze my eyes shut just as I hear a gunshot. No. *No.* This isn't happening.

I'm terrified to open my eyes and discover my husband lying on the sofa, a bullet hole in his head. I crack them open, and Noah is still sitting up. It doesn't appear he's been shot in the head. He looks fine.

Then I hear a gurgling sound coming from the ground. I look down—Warner is on the floor, gripping his neck, which is gushing blood. I stare down at him, my heart pounding. What just happened?

"I am so sorry, sweetie." Lindsay is standing over him, her brows knitted together. "But your story was just too complicated. And the police have your fingerprints on file. I just couldn't take the risk of being associated with you."

Warner coughs up blood. He looks like he's trying to say something, but he can't.

"Two people can't keep a secret," she says. "Not unless one of them is dead. It's just a fact. I always work alone."

I watch in horror as Warner's eyes roll up in their sockets. He's dead. She just killed him.

"So," Lindsay says briskly. She seems utterly unconcerned that she just killed a man, and that chills me. Who is this woman? I thought I knew her better than anyone else. "Here's the deal. I met Warner on a dating site, and my bad, he turned out to be a psychopath. He killed all of us, but I managed to survive by playing dead." She smiles benevolently. "So you get to be innocent victims. That's your gift if you behave yourselves and don't try anything funny."

Try anything funny? What am I supposed to do? *She's* got the gun. Of course, Warner dropped his rifle on the ground, but Lindsay knows better than anyone that I would have no idea what to do with that thing. I doubt Noah does either. Except…

Where's that Swiss Army knife?

I see Noah's right hand is in his pocket now. Lindsay doesn't seem to have noticed. Does he have the knife in there? If he has it, we've got a chance. If he doesn't…well…

"So," Lindsay says, "which one of you would like to go first?"

Oh God. Please let Noah have that knife.

I take a breath, stalling for time. "Lindsay, you've got to understand, what I did with Jack…it just happened. I didn't mean for it to happen."

"Right." She snorts. "That's the same thing my father said."

"Your father was an asshole," I say. She jerks her head back, but I push on. "I remember when he died, we stayed up all night talking about him. Do you remember that?"

Lindsay sneers. "It was a long time ago,"

"Well, *I* remember." I look her in the eyes. "You told me about how badly he treated your mother. How he was never there for your family. That you always felt like you weren't good enough for him."

Lindsay lowers her gun a millimeter. "Yeah, well…"

"You and I…" I swallow hard. "We were always there for each other. Every time I needed you, you were there for me, Lindsay. I mean, you were my maid of honor. You're my kids' godmother. When I thought you were dead…"

She looks at me for a moment. "When you thought I died and you wanted to stay behind, I almost couldn't go through with it. I…I honestly didn't think you would care enough."

"What are you talking about? Of course I care!"

As the words are coming out of my mouth, I realize how much I mean them. When I thought Lindsay was dead, it was like my whole world was falling apart. Clearly, she has much deeper issues than I ever thought possible. I mean, I always knew she was a little out there. But I never suspected she could be capable of this.

Part of me still doesn't believe it.

"Lindsay," I choke out, "we can figure this out. I'll do whatever it takes to get you out of this."

Of course, there isn't really a way out of it. Three people are dead. But Lindsay's face softens, and she lowers her gun. I let out a breath. "I don't want to kill you, Claire." She shakes her head. "I really don't. But you have to understand…" She lifts her eyes. "You know too much. I can't trust you to keep my secrets."

And then she starts to raise the gun again. Oh my God. This is really happening. In a second, I'm going to be joining Warner on the floor.

My eyes flutter shut, bracing myself. But a split second later, I hear Lindsay scream, and my eyes fly open. Noah is behind her, and his Swiss Army knife is sticking out of her right shoulder. The sleeve of her pink T-shirt quickly darkens with blood as the gun tumbles to the floor.

"Claire!" Noah snaps at me. "Get the gun! Now!"

I know what he's telling me to do. I've got to pick up the gun. But I feel like I'm in a trance. I can't move. "But…"

"Claire! Get! The! Gun!"

His shouts snap me out of my trance. I scramble for the gun on the floor, although I've never held a gun before and I'm not entirely sure how to. I'm only vaguely sure the barrel isn't pointed in my direction.

Lindsay sinks to the ground as the crimson stain on her T-shirt continues to grow. I try to hold the gun steady, but my hands won't stop shaking.

"Claire," she croaks, "put the gun down. I know you're not going to shoot me."

Noah glares at her. He's got the Swiss Army knife in his right hand and it's slick with her blood. "Claire might not." He firmly pulls the gun from my hands, and I let him. "But I sure would."

I look over at him. He's got Lindsay's gun and he's pointing it at her. His hands are surprisingly steady, considering I've never seen him aim a gun before. I believe he would shoot her. He would do what he has to do to defend us both. After all, he promised me he would get us home.

"Are you okay with handling that?" I ask quietly.

Noah nods briskly. "I can handle it. Just get away from her."

I feel sick as I look down at my former best friend, lying on the ground of the cabin. Her face is the color of a sheet. I don't know if she's going to make it through this. I'm not sure if I hope she does or doesn't. She wipes her forehead and smears blood all over her hair.

"I'm sorry, Claire," she whispers.

Noah puts his hand on my shoulder. He gently turns me away from Lindsay so I don't have to see the life drain out of her.

EPILOGUE

CLAIRE

Emma launches herself at me so rapidly I nearly fall over. If I thought she was clinging hard to me before I left for the trip, it's about a million times harder now. But this time, I'm clinging to her just as hard.

I look over to my right, and the usually reserved Aidan is clinging to Noah. Any second, we're probably going to have to trade kids. Although I'd really like to hug both at once. I didn't think I'd see either of them ever again.

When we were an hour away from the house, I called my sister to bring the kids by. Now she's standing in the middle of our living room, looking a little misty eyed herself. She knew the first night that something was wrong, but nobody would start searching until the second day, when we missed our reservation.

"Glad you made it back, sis," Penny says.

I look up from my Emma hug and hold out my arms. She comes in for a hug on top of Emma. And then Aidan wants to be part of it too. Eventually, all five of us are hugging together. It's a little ridiculous, but it makes me happy. There were moments when I was so sure I would never get to hug any of these people again.

The police arrived only ten minutes after Noah stabbed Lindsay. Warner had a device to block our cell phone signals, but before Noah could figure out how to turn it off, the police were there. Lindsay had placed a tearful call earlier, saying that Warner was threatening them with a gun and to come right away. She had set the stage.

According to the police, Warner's real name was Donald Regis. He was wanted in two other states in connection with multiple murders. If everything had gone according to plan for Lindsay, he would have served as the perfect scapegoat. Especially since he was dead and couldn't defend himself.

The man who owned the cabin was a recluse named Paul Duffy. Lindsay and Warner had never met him before, but his cabin was in a perfect location. That's why they murdered him. Bad luck on his part.

Lindsay, on the other hand, survived. She was still breathing when the paramedics took her away. But she'll be serving significant time for four murders. Well, *at least* four murders. It's not clear how many people Lindsay killed throughout her life. I'm not sure we'll ever know.

Jack and Michelle are dead. Just before we left, one of the officers reported they found Michelle's body. She was stabbed to death—there was no wild animal involved. Lindsay and her boyfriend made all those claw marks themselves in advance to throw us off their scent. They used a magnet on Jack's compass to lead us exactly where they wanted us to go.

Noah and I might have survived, but nothing will bring Jack and Michelle back. Every time I think about it, I feel a sting of sadness.

Why would Lindsay do it? Yes, I always knew she was a little odd. She was passionate about right and wrong, especially when it came to the opposite sex. Of course, when I looked back, all my memories of her took on a new light. When we were in college, we were sharing some beers outside a bar, and some guy approached us and wouldn't take no for an answer. Lindsay broke her beer bottle against the wall and shoved the jagged edge close to the guy's neck. He took off quickly after that.

I always admired Lindsay for that one. I never would have had the nerve to threaten some creep with a broken beer bottle. But now, when I look back at that night, I remember the gleam in her eyes and how much she seemed to enjoy seeing him squirm.

And then, of course, there was Ted. My ex-boyfriend who I caught cheating on me. How furious she had been on my behalf. I was furious too. I remember her ranting, *He should pay for doing this to you.* But I never imagined she would feel the need to exact justice.

In the end, I disappointed Lindsay just like everyone else did. Maybe I didn't deserve to die, but she was right that I did something terrible. I'm not sure if I'll ever forgive myself, even though Noah has forgiven me.

As Emma clings to my hips, I wonder how I'm going to tell the kids that Aunt Lindsay is going to jail for the rest of her life. And that she's the one who tried to kill their mother. They both adored Lindsay—honestly, I think Aidan had a crush. Maybe I can make up some creative lies.

"I missed you guys so much," I say.

Noah reaches out and squeezes my hand. I feel a rush of affection for the man who only a few days ago I would have said I hated. I thought he and I were done. I believed when we returned home, we would be talking about how to split our house and our bank accounts.

"It's good to be home," he says.

I squeeze his hand back.

———————

Emma and I are making dinner for the family tonight. Noah suggested ordering in pizza, but after everything we've been through, I feel like a home-cooked meal is in order. Unfortunately, we don't have much food in the house because we had been planning to be gone for a week, but there's enough to throw together a casserole.

"Do you need any help here?" Noah asked before he went to play Aidan's favorite video game with him. But he didn't ask in the begrudging way he used to. He asked like he really wanted to help.

"No, we're good," I told him.

"Are you sure?" He slid his hands around my waist and pulled me close to him. "Because whatever you need…"

I smiled. "We'll be fine. But maybe later this week, you and I can have a night out."

He leaned in to kiss me. "You read my mind."

So now Emma and I are throwing together a casserole. She's scooping out the contents of a can of cream of mushroom soup into my large pan, and I'm stirring the egg noodles on the stove. The oven is preheating itself to four hundred degrees.

"I love cream of mushroom soup," Emma comments. She digs her spoon into the soup and takes a mouthful of it.

I cringe. Is it okay for a kid to eat raw soup? "Emma…"

"But, Mommy, it's yum!"

No way that's "yum." But whatever. It won't kill her.

"I'm so glad you're home," Emma says. "I *told* you something bad was going to happen on the trip."

Once again, Emma's premonition came true. Well, sort of. "You said a monster was going to eat us."

She eats another spoonful of cold soup. "Well, I got worried because Daddy said he was going to take that hike."

"Hike? You mean go fishing."

"Nuh uh." She licks soup off her fingers. "Hike. In the woods."

"Are…are you sure?"

She nods. "With Uncle Jack."

I shake my head. "No, *I* was going to go on a hike with Uncle Jack."

"Daddy was too," Emma insists. "I heard them talking about it on the phone. They were going on a hike, just the two of them."

Emma is looking up at me with her wide brown eyes. She has a great memory, and if she says she heard Noah and Jack planning a solo hike together, I'm sure that's exactly what happened. And there's nothing wrong with that. After all, that's why we were going out to that remote inn. So we could hike and fish and whatever.

So why does this revelation make me feel uneasy?

I wanted to do whatever it took to get you back.

I never asked Noah why he had that Swiss Army knife in his pocket. Or why he stole it back from the drawer. It seemed so unimportant after the fact. And maybe I didn't want to hear the answer.

It occurs to me that our luggage is still in the car. The police seized everything that belonged to Jack, Michelle, Lindsay, and Warner, but they let us keep our own stuff. When we got home, we were too excited to see the kids to think about our bags. Everything is still sitting there.

The timer goes off to signify that the egg noodles are cooked. I shut off the heat on the stove and drain the noodles into a colander. A puff of steam rises from the noodles.

"Hey, Emma," I say. "I'm going to run out to the garage to get our bags. Can you keep an eye on things in the kitchen?"

Emma nods solemnly. "Yes."

"And…?"

"I won't touch the stove."

I kiss her forehead. "Good girl."

We have an attached garage, big enough for two cars. I grab my car keys and slip through the door to the garage, which is pitch-black. I flick on the light, but it's still only a dim glow. My minivan is sitting next to Noah's Prius. I hit the button on my key fob and my car lights up.

Noah's bag is the smaller green one. I feel around the edges, searching for the zipper. I'm not entirely sure why I'm doing this or what I'm hoping to find. I suppose I just want reassurance. I want to know for sure that the private hike Noah and Jack were planning together was nothing more than that.

I unzip the length of the luggage and throw it open. His shirts and pants are folded haphazardly inside, with sock balls scattered throughout. There's nothing scary or unusual in this luggage. It looks like a typical guy's messy luggage.

I let out a breath of relief.

Just to be sure, I start feeling around the clothing. His shirts feel soft under my fingers. I don't know what I'm looking for. A gun? Another knife? In any case, I don't find anything. Not that I'm surprised.

Anyway, I should probably bring our luggage inside. Knowing my husband, if I don't do it, he'll probably let them sit there in the trunk for the next several weeks. So I grab his luggage and pull it out of the trunk. I also grab his sweatshirt, which he had been wearing out in the woods and abandoned in the trunk. That one definitely needs to be washed, since I didn't wash it out in the sink.

Except when I drop the sweatshirt down on his luggage, it pings.

I pick up the gray sweatshirt, curious what would have made that noise. I unzip one of the pockets on the side. Then I shake it out.

To my surprise, a little silver brick falls out.

I recognize it instantly. It's one of the really strong refrigerator magnets Noah bought when Emma's and Aidan's drawings kept falling off the fridge. But why did he have a magnet in his sweatshirt? What had he been planning to do with it?

I wanted to do whatever it took to get you back.

It's silly to be suspicious. Warner probably put it there. They were planning to frame him, after all. Or did they?

I wanted to do whatever it took to get you back.

Anything.

"Claire?" Noah's voice echoes from just outside the garage. I shove the magnet quickly back inside his shirt. "You in the garage?"

255

"Yes, just getting our luggage out of the car!" I call back.

I drop the sweatshirt back down on his bag just as he opens the door to the garage and finds me standing by his luggage. He holds up his hands. "You don't have to worry about that, Claire. You're cooking dinner. The least I can do is lug our bags upstairs."

Last week, this would have been an argument in which I accused him of procrastinating every chore until I couldn't stand it and had to do them myself. But things are different now. "I don't mind," I say.

"I promise, I'm on top of it." He steps into the garage and joins me in front of the trunk. He lifts his dirty sweatshirt off the luggage and drapes it over his arm. "You shouldn't have to deal with my dirty clothes. I can wash this myself."

"Oh," I murmur. "Well, I usually do the laundry."

He grabs my wrist to pull me close to him. "It's the least I can do. I just want you to know how much I appreciate you." He kisses me softly on the lips. "I'm not going to screw it up again."

I try to relax as Noah kisses me again, but it's hard not to wonder what exactly he had been planning for this trip. If Lindsay hadn't intervened, did Noah intend to bring Jack out to the woods and get him disoriented? Would Jack have suffered a stab wound while hiking? Is it possible my husband would do something like that?

I'd like to think he wouldn't. I'd like to think there's a perfectly reasonable explanation for all of this. And anyway, he didn't kill Jack—Warner did. Why ask a question that will threaten our newfound happiness together?

Sometimes it's better not to know.

LINDSAY

Well, it didn't quite work out as I planned.

The DA is saying I'm looking at multiple consecutive life sentences, but my lawyer says there's a chance he'll get me off on an insanity defense. If that happens, I'll serve a few years in a nice quiet psychiatric hospital, then I'll be right back home. He said nobody will throw a pretty woman in jail for life. People are very superficial.

I think it's unlikely I'll get off on insanity though. Now that I've been caught, people are putting two and two together and figuring out what I've done in the past. All those other murders, although every single one of them was deserved. I thought I was so careful, but it turns out I left evidence behind. They will never let me go. I'll spend the rest of my life in this cold cell with this uncomfortable bed.

I have a lot of time to think in here.

What I keep thinking about are those last few moments in the cabin. I was so close. If only I hadn't turned my back on Noah. I had forgotten he had that Swiss Army knife, and I certainly didn't think he had it in him to use it. He only managed to do it because he thought I was going to shoot Claire. Nothing else could have motivated him. Despite what she did to him, he still loved her so much.

It's ironic because I was the one who gave him that knife. I did it while we were at the rest stop, while Claire was in the bathroom. I smiled helplessly at him and said I was scared to hold it because I might accidentally hurt myself. He took it without question. Men are so easy.

It was Warner's idea to put the magnet in Noah's sweatshirt, in that zippered pocket where he was unlikely to look. I took the magnet right off their refrigerator when I was visiting. All along, Noah was the one throwing off Jack's compass without even realizing it. Jack suspected it, and that's why he believed his best friend was trying to keep them lost in the woods for his own nefarious purposes.

That was back when Warner planned to pin it all on Noah. Of course, the magnet is still in there. Nestled inside the pocket of his dirty sweatshirt.

I wonder if Claire will find the magnet when she's doing the laundry. After all, she's the one who always washes the clothes—it's something she complains about constantly. She'll see it and she'll wonder. Wonder if there's more to Noah's story than he's letting on.

I know Claire so well—it will eat at her. They think they fixed their marriage, but that magnet will destroy them.

And they will finally get what they deserve.

READING GROUP GUIDE

1. In the first few chapters, who did you expect the anonymous narrator to be? How did your reasoning change as you read further?

2. Claire isn't sure when or why she started hating Noah. How do you cope with the many changes your partner will go through in a lifetime of marriage? How do we fall into unpleasant habits, and how can we reverse them?

3. Do you think Michelle would really destroy Jack in a divorce, or was that an excuse to keep Claire from wanting too much from their affair?

4. Have you ever had to read a paper map? How would you navigate without a phone or GPS?

5. Why does the group decide to leave the van and search together? If you had the same resources, what would be your strategy for getting help or finding the inn?

6. When Claire realizes how invested Lindsay is in her relationship with Warner, she backs off from criticizing him. If you thought that your friend was about to accept a proposal from someone like Warner, what would you do?

7. What makes a strong relationship? Why do the hardships throughout the book start to shore up Claire's relationship with Noah?

8. The anonymous narrator does not intervene in their mother's suicide attempt. Do you think that inaction constitutes murder?

9. What was your reaction when the anonymous narrator's identity was revealed? What kind of person did Lindsay define as "bad"? Do you think she's right about what will happen to Claire and Noah?

ACKNOWLEDGMENTS

I'm so thankful to all the supportive people in my life who help me through the painful editing process. Writing is a solitary process, but after that first draft, I need all the help I can get. I feel lucky to have all the support I get—friends and family who are always there to give me an opinion or more.

Thank you to my mother for the encouraging feedback and for helping me catch all those pesky typos. Thanks to Jen for the thorough critique and talking through it with me. Thanks to Kate for the great suggestions. Thanks to Rebecca for your great advice. Thanks to Ken and Greg for giving me the opinion of a guy. It's incredible to have that support in my life. And thanks to my writing group!

And as always, thank you to the rest of my family. Without your encouragement, none of this would be possible.

ABOUT THE AUTHOR

#1 Amazon, *USA Today*, and *Publishers Weekly* bestselling author Freida McFadden is a practicing physician specializing in brain injury. Freida's work has been selected as one of Amazon Editors' Best Books of the Year, and she has been a Goodreads Choice Award nominee. Her novels have been translated into more than thirty languages. Freida lives with her family and black cat in a centuries-old three-story home overlooking the ocean.